MARY CRAWFORD

Pieces

HIDDEN HEARTS BOOK 7

COPYRIGHT

HIDDEN BEAUTY SERIES

Until the Stars Fall from the Sky
So the Heart Can Dance
Joy and Tiers
Love Naturally
Love Seasoned
Love Claimed
If You Knew Me (and other silent musings) (novella)
Jude's Song
The Price of Freedom (novella)
Paths Not Taken
Dreams Change (novella)
Heart Wish (100% charity release)
Tempting Fate
The Letter
The Power of Will

HIDDEN HEARTS SERIES

Identity of the Heart

Sheltered Hearts

Hearts of Jade

Port in the Storm (novella)

Love is More Than Skin Deep

Tough

Rectify

Pieces (a crossover novel)

Hearts Set Free

Freedom (a crossover novel)

The Long Road to Love (novella)

Love and Injustice (Protection Unit)

Out of Thin Air (Protection Unit)

Soul Scars (Protection Unit)

OTHER WORKS:

The Power of Dictation

Vision of the Heart

#AmWriting: A Collection of Letters to Benefit The
Wayne Foundation

DEDICATION

This book is dedicated to all
law enforcement officers.
Thanks for putting yourself on the line
when the stakes are high.

CHAPTER ONE

KATIE

"Mom! Do you have to do that? It hurts!" I declare as I rub my scalp. "Ouch! Are those supposed to be drilling a hole in my head?"

Carolyn Ashford takes a moment to study me as if I am a precious work of art. "Yes, actually, they are. It'll be worth it. Today is your wedding day! Besides, you only get to do this once. Suck it up — the pain is only temporary."

I hardly recognize myself in the mirror. This perfectly coiffed, sophisticated woman looking back at me is not who I am. I am a tomboy with a klutzy streak. I can't believe my mom is letting me use the veil my grandmother wore. She knows how I am. I'll probably do irreparable damage to our priceless family heirloom before the day is done.

My mom catches my gaze in the mirror. "Katelyn, you look stunning. I can't believe you are so grown-up." She straightens my veil and jams another bobby pin into my head.

I grimace as my stomach lurches. "Thanks, Mom. I don't feel like a real person. It's like I'm staring at a live version of Bridal Barbie. It's a little surreal."

"Don't be silly. You look lovely." My mom rubs my shoulders in a comforting gesture.

A sudden urge hits and I groan. "Really? This has to happen right now?" I look at my mother with desperation as I plead, "Please tell me how to pee in this thing. I swear I have the world's worst timing."

"Relax, it's jitters. Every bride gets them. You'll be fine."

"Mom, I'm not kidding. I really have to go to the restroom. If I don't, things could get ugly."

My mom rolls her eyes. "All right, go ahead and I'll meet you there. I need to turn off all the curling irons. Pastor Henderson would never forgive me if I burn down his lovely little church while trying to get you married."

I tuck my cellphone into my garter and force the most sincere smile I can muster at my mom. Making my way down the narrow hallway in the historic church proves to be a feat. I will be so glad when I can change back into my cutoffs and halter top. This fancy stuff is for the birds.

As I am fighting with my train in front of the bathroom door, the door to the men's bathroom opens, and my fiancé emerges wearing his tails and cummerbund. His ascot is perfectly arranged.

I gasp. "Vinnie! It's totally bad luck for you to see me. Don't look!"

"That's a stupid superstition. I don't know why you didn't let me choose your dress. It would've made much more sense for me to do it. You have the fashion sense of a hyperactive four-year-old."

"Ouch … way to make me feel good."

"Katelyn, didn't we talk about you wearing a white dress? I specifically said that's the color I wanted."

I bristle at his criticism. Stiffly, I respond, "You don't get to decide what I wear on my wedding day. You should love me even if I go up the aisle buck naked."

"My family has certain expectations about how a bride should look."

"Really now?" I spit as my anger grows.

He looks down his nose at me. "I suppose this dress is nice enough for most people. But to me, it looks yellowed and old. What are you wearing on your head? It is not remotely appropriate for this decade."

I pick up my train and hit my butt on the door to open it. "If you'll excuse me, I need to visit the facilities. We'll talk about this later."

Once I escape into the safety of the bathroom, I take a chair and block the door. A chunk of my elaborate hairdo falls down into my face and seems to break my dam of emotions and I start to cry. Frustrated, I snag a paper towel and try to mop up the tears flowing down my face. I catch a glimpse at my now disheveled self in the mirror. The illusion of perfection is gone. Then it hits me. I don't want to marry Vinnie. He was once my Vinnie-the-Pooh, but after the newness wore off of our relationship, my cute boyfriend became ugly as heck on the inside.

I breathe deeply to slow down my pulse, which is beating at roughly the same rate as the wings of a hummingbird.

I've never felt so out of control. When did I actually lose control of my life? Maybe it was when my brother John was in his accident and became blind. Or maybe it was when not one, not two, not three, but five candidates from the police academy who were all less qualified than I was each got better paying jobs. Then again, it could have all started when I got shot. That kind of thing has a way of waking a person up.

Someone pounds on the bathroom door, so I yell, "What?"

"Get out here. I wasn't done talking to you," Vinnie snarls.

"Too bad, I am completely done talking to you. Go away."

"You can't be. You are my wife. If I want to talk to you, we will talk. You'll do as I say."

If I was wavering before, his comment is enough to seal his fate. I don't care if he is my betrothed. *No one* gets to talk to me that way. I use my indignation to announce, "I am not your wife yet. It has become abundantly clear, only an insane person would marry you. Since I am not crazy, I'm not marrying you today … or any other day."

"Oh no you don't! I paid good money for this custom tuxedo, and you're darn well going to marry me. Stop being such a baby."

I groan as I think about all the money I'm about to throw down the drain. I tried to keep my wedding expenses to a minimum, but this stuff is horrendously expensive. My dad will probably have kittens … *and* bunnies.

He pounds on the door again and warns, "Katiedyd —"

"Don't try to sweet talk me with cute pet names," I interrupt. "I don't know if you didn't hear me, or what, but I said go away. Go home. I am not marrying you. *Now or ever.*"

My *former* fiancé, who considers himself to be the epitome of suave and debonair, kicks the bathroom door so hard he puts a hole in it. For a moment, his shiny patent leather shoe is stuck in the door. I hear a string of expletives as he pulls his foot out.

"It's not fair. You promised to marry me and now you are going to embarrass me in front of all my friends. I have potential clients out in the audience today. This will make me look terrible. How do you expect me to explain this?"

"How about admitting you are such a controlling creep your fiancée is concerned enough she doesn't want to marry you?"

"Very funny. Most people can handle what I dish out. Just because you're weak doesn't mean I'm wrong."

"Trust me, no one should have to deal with what you dish out — least of all your spouse. So, *this* woman will not be your wife."

"I thought you loved me," he whines.

"I thought I did too. However, it seems I have fallen in love with some idealized model of the guy I wish you were instead of the person you really are. I don't much like the person you actually are. I'm not going to marry you and have you belittle every choice I make in life. As I recently learned, life is far too short to live with regrets. Marrying you would be the *biggest* regret of my life."

"Not fair! I sprung for all the best restaurants, parties, and vacations. I treated you like a princess. You should be grateful."

"Perhaps you should spend a little less *money* and spend a little more *time* on your personality and the way you treat people."

"So help me God! If you don't walk down the aisle with me, there will be some serious repercussions," he threatens.

It suddenly dawns on me I am not the only person who's different today. I sure as heck don't recognize the person screaming at me from the other side of the door. I wonder whatever happened to the charming, debonair guy I met?

"Well, it won't be the first time I faced something serious. It probably won't be the last either. You know, I am a cop."

"I know; I planned to fix that little inconvenience so you wouldn't be anymore."

I sigh as I rest my head against the door jamb. "I don't want to give up my job as a police officer. I worked hard to get certified. It disturbs me you think you can direct the kind of person I am. That's not the way a true marriage works."

"Katie, think about what you're doing. If you ruin your chance with me today, you'll never get another one."

"I'm counting on it. Please go away." I sigh as my adrenaline burst passes and the gravity of the situation sets in.

Vincent pounds on the bathroom door. His blows are hard enough it splinters by the hinges. "I won't let you do this to me, you little twat. You will marry me today whether you want to or not. As planned."

When the wood cracks again, I reach under my layers and layers of petticoats to retrieve my cell phone. I hit the speed dial and call in the cavalry.

"Hi, how is the blushing bride today?" Cody Erickson, my partner, answers.

"10-2 women's restroom," I whisper as the pounding on the door gets more intense.

"Only you could call a code at your own wedding, Ashford," Cody mutters. "I'm coming. Do you want me to come in hot?"

"I don't think so. But the suspect is agitated."

"Is he 10-12?"

"Good question. He could definitely qualify as mentally disturbed today."

"10-4, I'm on my way."

After what seems like forever, I hear Cody's deep voice command, "Step away from the door."

Astonishingly, Vinnie replies, "Who is going to make me?"

The man must be touched today because the answer should be self-explanatory. Cody is pretty intimidating. His stare alone can make you wither.

"I am … and if you don't comply, a bunch of my friends will help me," Cody answers.

"You have no right to interfere. This is a matter between my wife and me."

"I think you're mistaken. Officer Ashford is not your wife."

"Whether she has a ring on her finger or not, she is mine," Vinnie snaps. "She promised to marry me and she's going to. I won't be made a fool of in front of all my friends, family, and colleagues."

"I don't think that's the way it works. I don't think

that's the way any of this works," Cody comments. "Last time I checked, indentured servitude was illegal. If the woman does not want to marry you, you need to man up and deal with it."

"You don't know what it's like to be humiliated like this," Vinnie argues.

"As a matter of fact, I do. It doesn't feel great. It's not enough reason to make threats and generally be a jerk."

"But I —"

"But, nothing. The lady asked you to leave."

"This is my wedding. I have a right to be here."

Cody yells through the door at me. "Hey, K … Didn't you tell me you ended up renting the church and paying for catering?"

I practically whimper. "Don't remind me. My day is already crappy enough."

"I know, it royally bites. However, in this case, it will help me do my job."

"You're supposed to be here as my friend not in your official capacity. I'm sorry to drag you into the middle of this."

"Not a problem. As partners, we have each other's back."

"Are you sure that's all you've had of my fiancé?" Vinnie asks pointedly.

"Real charmer you found here," Cody comments dryly.

A tear slides down my face as I say, "I know that *now*. In the beginning, it seemed so good. I should've known it was too good to be true. Vinnie, I'm sorry but this is never gonna work out between us. Please don't make this a bigger scene than it needs to be. If you do, Cody and the rest of my squad members will have to arrest you, which would put your job at risk. Please don't make me do that."

"Yeah, you and your buddies probably planned this whole thing. You know, the thin blue line —"

"Get a clue!" I yell, blowing the hair out of my eyes. "I didn't plan anything except to get married to a nice guy. Clearly, the nice guy was in my imagination. Since you're not who you presented yourself to be, I don't feel obligated to marry you."

I hear my mom's voice enter the fray. "Oh dear, this isn't what we planned for."

"Can you believe it? She plans to ditch me in front of everyone."

"I only see Cody," my mom logically points out.

"Well, everyone will know I got dumped on the church steps. What does that say about me?"

"You're a chauvinistic asshat?" I yell through the door.

"You better be thankful there is a door between me and you. If there wasn't, I would make you pay for that remark."

"Watch yourself!" Cody warns. "If I hear one more threat against Ms. Ashford, I'll take official action. My partner doesn't want me to, so I suggest you take everyone's advice and leave."

"What about my friends and family?"

"We'll handle them. You need to go."

"Fine! I always thought you were a sniveling twit anyway," Vinnie pouts. "Good riddance!"

For a few moments, I hear nothing and then Cody says through the door, "You can stand down now. He's gone."

Visceral relief travels through my body. I sag against the wall.

"Can you let me in?" my mom asks.

"One moment Mom, I have to move the barricade."

"I don't know what happened," my mom says as I open the door to let her in. "One moment you were on your way to get married and now you look like you did when you were about to run a race in high school."

I slump down in the chair I just moved. "Yeah, that about sums it up. I need to run as hard as I can to get away from this whole situation. I'm sorry, Mom. I'm not up to telling you any more about it." I dab away my tears and blow my nose.

"Aww honey," my mom says as she takes in my appearance.

"Can you do me a favor and let everybody know there won't be a wedding? Encourage them to stay and eat though because the foods already paid for. Tell my crew the party's on me. They can even take it back to their station houses if they want to. Lord knows, the family can only eat so much food."

"You have always been a puzzle to me. You're so impulsive on one hand, yet so practical on the other. When you're ready, you know where I live. I'll fix tea and cookies and we'll hash this out."

"Thanks, Mom. I'm so sorry to put you and Dad

through all this."

My mom looks regal in her mother-of-the-bride outfit, but she ignores our wedding garb as she comes over and gives me a gentle hug. "All your dad and I ever wanted is for you to be happy. I might have made different choices, but I'm not you. Be forewarned though, I expect your father will have some choice comments to make about all of this."

"Mom, I can't handle it right now — maybe someday, but not now."

"Go! I'll go run interference with your dad." She bustles my train.

"I love you, Mom." I claim one more hug. "You are the best."

"I don't claim to understand you, but I love you too."

"What's a pretty girl like you doing in a joint like this?" The bartender asks as he slides another whiskey in front of me.

"I'd rather not talk about it." I throw the veil over my shoulder for what seems like the billionth time.

"Oh come on. You can't do that to us," the sexy bartender protests. "It's not every day I get to serve a bride in her full regalia."

"Trust me. It's false advertising. I'm not really a bride."

"So you're in a play or something?"

"Oh, I'm in a play all right. Everything I thought was true about my life turned out to be fiction. It's like one huge badly acted play." I take a long drink. Instinctively, I exhale roughly as the alcohol singes my throat.

"Hey, you might want to take it easy, JD is lethal."

"I don't know where you got the idea I'm a lightweight drinker. Did I order anything fruity or pink? No, I did not. I ordered Jack Daniels."

"Sorry, I meant no offense. I get a lot of inexperienced drinkers — Gainesville being a college town and all. Many people don't know what they can handle. They see a television ad showing someone cool drinking the hard stuff and think they can handle anything."

"I'm a ways away from twenty-one. I've been drinking with the guys longer than you can imagine. I can drink some of them under the table," I boast.

"Alrighty then." He shrugs. "I'll leaving you with a glass of ice water in case you want to slow down a bit."

"I have no intention of slowing down. I would like to obliterate today from my memory banks forever. My friend Jack Daniels wants to help me. So, if you don't mind, we need a few moments alone."

Chapter Two

Logan

"What do you think the story is there?" I ask Nick as I observe the beautiful, elegant woman slam another glass down on the bar.

"I don't know — but she obviously hates Restless Heart." He shrugs nonchalantly.

I take a drink of my beer. "Yeah, true. She was pretty rough on the jukebox. Fortunately, the bartender was able to distract her from her path of destruction."

"Maybe she doesn't like country music," Nick suggests.

"I don't think she's anti-country; she's belting out other songs. It's clear she knows every single Martina McBride song."

"True. Do you think she'd be impressed by the likes of us? I mean, being security for Aidan O'Brien is something at least."

"You can take a run at her if you want to, but I'm steering clear. She doesn't look like she's in a mood to talk to anything with a Y chromosome today."

"For a former military guy, you're a big chicken,"

Nick teases with a chuckle.

"Sometimes, it's prudent to stay out of the war zone."

Nick shrugs. "Nothing ventured, nothing gained. You want to watch my six?"

"Actually, I can think of a million things I'd rather be doing than watching you get shot down."

"Come on, it'll be educational for you. I bet you don't get turned down very often. Consider it a learning opportunity," he responds with a wink as he heads over to the bar. "Lucky for us, we've been nursing our drinks today. I have a feeling this might be a complicated mission."

For reasons unknown to me, I am watching him like a lost puppy. My gut tells me this is a terrible idea, but Nick tends to charge right into situations without doing proper recognizance. He needs someone to watch his six. Reluctantly, I get up and follow him.

When he notices me beside him, he smirks. "I knew you couldn't resist a damsel in distress."

I frown at his words. The remark hits a little close to home. Yet, out of the corner of my eye I notice the bartender has placed another drink in front of her. Three by my count. She is a little slip of a thing. If she weighs a buck-o-two, I'd be surprised.

I sigh. "I hate it when you're right. I think we need to intervene — otherwise, our Princess Bride might end up in the ER with alcohol toxicity."

"Yeah, I was thinking the same thing. My dad died of alcohol poisoning. It's not something to mess with. I figured a little flirting might get us closer."

"I'll leave that to you. I'm not so smooth with the ladies. It's been a while for me."

"Come on … with all those groupies around Aidan and Jude, are you telling me there no one has caught your eye?"

"What'd I tell you on the day you started working for me? Never pursue the groupies."

"I hear you. Still, some of them are total knockouts."

"Yeah, they knock out your common sense."

We work our way through the crowded bar and finally reach her. Fortunately for us, the barstools on either side of the woman are free.

Nick scoots a bowl of peanuts closer. "You know, Darlin', peanuts are good with Jack."

"No, thanks. Penis make me sick," she remarks.

"I don't recall offering mine; but here are some legumes."

"Well aren't you a fancy English teacher? I told you I don't like peanuts. They make me puke."

I can barely disguise my grin. "Actually, that's not *quite* what you said."

"Huh? What are you talking about?" she asks with a puzzled expression.

"Don't mind my friend here, he's being a jerk," Nick responds as he studies her carefully.

"All men are jerks. Well, maybe not my brother—"

"I'm sorry you feel that way. Let me introduce myself. My name is Nick Weston, and this is my boss, Logan Anthony."

"You got two first names? If you're making up a

pseudonym for yourself, at least try to be creative," she challenges me.

"I can assure you it's not made up. Where I'm from, Logan means hollow."

"Hollow, kinda like this conversation. Have you seen how many times guys have tried to pick me up tonight? You gotta do better than the origins of your name. Anybody can look up random facts on Wikipedia."

"Touché. However, I've got the driver's license and DNA tests to prove who I am."

"I'm sorry," she says with a shrug. "It's an occupational hazard. Sometimes, I'm way more skeptical than I need to be."

"Occupational hazard?" I raise an eyebrow as I look at her attire.

"Oh, stop with the stink eye," she answers as she catches my gaze. "I do *not* always dress this way. In fact, I would go as far as to say I'm a arbitration."

"Whoa-kay, I think it's time to slow down on these," Nick exclaims as he reaches in and slides her drink away.

"Why'd you do that? I'm not even close to a drunk and disorderly."

"Something tells me you just mangled the English language in a way which probably isn't typical for you when you're sober. We're just watching out for you."

"Knock it off. If I wanted to be controlled, I would've married the wind-bag."

She looks up at the bartender in alarm as she blurts, "I don't feel so well."

The bartender hands me a garbage can, which I put in front of her. She promptly loses her lunch, and probably her breakfast and dinner from the night before.

"Exactly what I'm talking about, Darlin'. You need to take better care of yourself. Jack will do a number on you."

"No, that's not the Jack Daniels talking. I thought about my ex-fiancé and all the problems I created today."

"Maybe it's not so bad," Nick tries to comfort.

"Tell that to all the people who were waiting for me to get married at the church. I let everyone down, including my parents. They're probably totally disappointed in me."

"I'm sorry." I reach across the bar and grab a stack of napkins. I dip one in my water glass as I wipe the vomit off her face.

"What's your address? I'm calling a cab to take you home," I say. "By the way, what's your name?"

"My name is Katelyn, but my friends call me Katie. I can't go home. Vinnie is really, really, *really* mad at me. He threatened to make me marry him. I'm scared of what he might do."

"Who is Vinnie?" I ask even though I have a strong, abiding hunch I already know.

"He was supposed to be my groom today until he put his butthole-ish tendencies on full display. I don't know what I was thinking … I should've realized it before today."

"Sometimes, we only see what we want to see in a relationship. But, hey, at least you discovered it before you actually made it down the aisle," Nick offers in support.

"I suppose you're right. But it doesn't change the fact I'm scared to go home. I don't know where to go because he knows how to find me everywhere."

"Did he threaten violence against you?" I ask.

"Not in so many words, but he did threaten some sort of retaliation. The cop in me is worried enough … I don't want to take any chances."

"So, what are you going to do?" Nick asks.

Katelyn shrugs, "I guess wait it out until closing time. Then, I'll find a quiet place to sleep off my drunk. The park has nice benches, maybe I'll end up there"

"With all due respect, I think you are exchanging one potential danger for another. How would you like a hotel room?"

She looks at me skeptically before she answers, "You know, even drunk, I know a very bad pick up line when I hear it. Besides, it's not nice to take advantage of someone in my condition."

"Listen, no strings attached. I want you to be safe."

"Safe?" she repeats with a frown. "I don't think I remember the meaning of the word *safe*. It has been years since I felt safe."

"Anything we can help with?" Nick asks.

"No, not unless you can turn back time. If you could turn back time, you could make sure I didn't get shot, and I didn't kill someone. Or if you want to go back even further, you could prevent the accident that blinded my big brother."

"You have no idea how much I empathize. I'd like to be able to turn back time too. Sadly, life doesn't work that way."

"Yeah, it'd be nice to be un-shot too," she comments with a slight sway.

"I know from personal experience; it hurts to be shot. I'm sorry you went through it. What happened in your case?"

"You mean you didn't see it splattered all over the news? I have no personal life now. Every part of my past has been raked over and exposed for the entire world to see."

"Nope, sorry. We missed the whole saga. Nick and I are from Oregon."

"What are you doing in Florida? You're an awfully long way from home. Surely there are drunk chicks to be picked up in your local bars."

"I, for one, am not picking you up. In answer to your other question, Nick and I provide security for Aidan O'Brien. He's here in Florida for a series of concerts. We happened to have some downtime."

Katelyn openly scoffs. "I'm with the band? I would've expected you guys to come up with something a little more original."

"Not picking you up …" I correct again as I pull my wallet out of my back pocket and show her my driver's license and business card.

"Wow, you really do have two first names. Anybody can easily get stuff printed off the Internet though. I was part of an investigation about a case of cat-fishing, and I learned everything I ever wanted to know about identity theft."

I rake my hand through my hair in frustration. "Look, you want to call my boss? He'll be happy to verify I'm the chief of security for him and Nick here is one of my employees."

Katelyn laughs out loud. "Oh sure! I'll get right on

calling Aidan O'Brien, Grammy winner. I actually saw him in concert in Vegas. I know what he sounds like."

"Great, it will be easier to prove to you I'm legit." I dig my phone out of the breast pocket of my jacket and dial Aidan's cell phone number.

"Sorry to bother you during your dinner out, but I need you to verify my employment," I instruct as Aidan answers the phone.

"Are you getting hassled by a fan?" Aidan asks.

"Something like that. Anyway, her name is Katelyn."

"Oh … I see."

"No, you don't see. I will explain later. Anyway, here she is," I hand Katelyn my phone. "Here's Aidan, he wants to talk to you," I say.

"Hello?" she answers skeptically as she moves her veil out of the way of the phone.

I can't hear what Aidan says to her, but her eyes widen appreciably.

"So, this isn't a joke?" she presses.

Katelyn listens for a few more seconds before she says, "Thank you for making that clear. I still can't believe I'm talking to you." She pushes the end button on my phone and hands it back to me.

"I'm so embarrassed. It seems you two guys are examples of a rare breed. I rarely run across men who tell the truth."

"I'm sorry, Darlin'," Nick mutters. "That's a shame. I hate it when other guys make us all look bad."

"I know it's not your fault, but in my book men universally suck!" Katelyn says before she passes out cold.

I reach out to catch her as she topples precariously on her barstool. However, Nick is closer and lifts her up in his arms.

"Is she here with anyone?" I ask the bartender.

"Nope, I've never seen her here before," he replies with a shake of his head.

Pulling out my wallet, I hand the bartender a business card and flash him my ID.

"If anyone comes looking for her, we'll be at the Sweetwater Branch Inn."

"I don't know if I should allow you to take her in this condition."

"Look, I used to provide medical services when I was in the military. I know what I'm doing. We won't hurt her. Do you think I would risk my employment for a quick lay?"

The bartender examines my business card more closely. "Holy shamole! You work for Aidan O'Brien."

"I not only work for Aidan, I am the head of security. I take my job very seriously. I've got sisters and if someone found my sisters in this kind of jam, I would hope someone would step up and help them," I argue.

"Okay, fine. I don't know what else to do with her because I don't know who she is. I can't have her passed out in the front of my bar. My manager would go ballistic. Don't do anything illegal, okay?"

"We weren't planning on it. I assure you."

I take the stethoscope out of my ears and remove the

blood pressure cuff from Katelyn. I study her closely before telling Nick, "Her vitals are good. She isn't clammy or blue and her respiration is normal. I don't think this is alcohol poisoning. I think she might be emotionally overwrought. She probably needs a little rest and some fluids."

"I've got some Gatorade up in my refrigerator. Do you want me to go grab it?"

"In a minute," I respond. "She can't sleep in this dress. Go next-door and grab a T-shirt and a pair of shorts from my dresser."

"They'll swim on her."

"Maybe so, but it's better than nothing. She'll probably be freaked out enough as it is when she wakes up. She doesn't need to wake up naked," I respond as I examine her dress. "Great; there are like a million and a half buttons on this dress."

"It's a wedding dress, did you expect anything else?" Nick replies with a smirk.

When I level a serious glance at him, he stutters, "I'll j-just go get those clothes for you."

While Nick is gone, I watched Katelyn's respiration and take her pulse again. I breathe a sigh of relief when everything checks out.

Nick returns with a pile of clothes. "I'm not sure which ones you wanted me to bring, so I brought a bunch."

"Try the red Under Armor; it's pretty tight fitting."

"Okay, here you go." Nick pulls out the running gear. "What are you going to do now?"

"You are the one who got us into this mess. I think

you should do what needs to be done."

"Me? I don't think so," Nick protests as he backs away. "You're the one who invited her back to the hotel. I was going for a little harmless flirting to make sure she was okay. She's your package now."

I heave a sigh. "We can't leave her like this. Her dress looks uncomfortable. I guess I'll start there."

"Whatever you say," Nick grimaces. "Stuff like this can get a guy like me into big trouble."

"I understand. I'll do the disrobing, but I need you to stand in front of her in case she falls forward."

After I gently pull Katelyn into a sitting position, I brace her against my knee as I kneel on the bed. Her head lolls forward, but she doesn't stir much. I am grateful when I discover after the first three buttons, there is a hidden zipper under the rest of them. As I unzip the dress and pull it down over her shoulders, I suck in a breath.

"Whoever her fiancé is, he was a fool," I mutter as I pull the dress down past her waist. She is wearing the sheerest corset I've ever seen. She looks like a model for Victoria's Secret.

"You aren't kidding. If I had a woman who would dress up like that for me, I would never let her go," Nick says.

"Let me have the shirt. I'll put it over her and then unhook the corset."

"I know it's the right thing to do, but it is a pity to cover all this gorgeousness."

"Weston, knock it off. We are performing a public service here. She'd probably be completely embarrassed if she knew we were gawking at her body."

Nick hands me the shirt. "10-4, but I'm not wrong. She is exquisite."

I place the shirt over her head and gently pull her arms through the arm holes. When I lift the back of the shirt to unhook the lacy lingerie, I notice the scarring under her shoulder blade.

"Wow! She wasn't just nicked by the bullet. From the looks of things, he nearly took her out."

"Okay, I've got the top down, let's pivot her around and work on pulling this dress down over her feet."

After we position her on the bed, I pull the dress down over her hips and I encounter the garter belt.

"I wondered why she didn't have a phone in the bar. Every person I know has their smart phone in their hand almost constantly." I pull the cell out of her garter belt.

I hand the phone off to Nick as I continue to work the dress over her legs and feet. Then, I awkwardly dress her in my shorts. She's like moving a sack of potatoes.

"Logan, she's got emergency contacts in her phone. According to her messages, one of those numbers has been trying to call her non-stop."

"Let me see," I comment as I pull the blankets over Katelyn. "What did she say her ex-fiancé's name was? We don't want to tip them off to her location."

"It was Vinnie or Victor or something," Nick responds as he examines her phone. "He's in here as a contact, but his number is different from the caller. It looks like this number belongs to a guy named John," Nick responds as he hands me the phone.

"Oh joy! Sometimes it sucks to be the supervisor. This won't be a fun call." I rub the back of my neck and try to work out a kink in my shoulder as I reluctantly pick up her cell phone.

Chapter Three

Katie

WHY DOES IT FEEL like my head is in a stupid vice? I reach up to check and encounter a handful of bobby pins strewn throughout my hair. Bobby pins? *Oh crap!* It wasn't all one big, awful nightmare.

A wave of nausea overtakes me and I frantically search for something to throw up in. There is a plastic ice bucket near me on the bed. For several minutes, I vomit so hard it feels like I'm tearing muscles in my rib cage. As I instinctively grab for my torso, I realize my wedding dress is gone. *Holy crap! Where the heck am I?* I frantically search my brain for answers, but come up with none. All my law enforcement instincts race to the surface. A million scenarios pass through my thoughts and none of them are good.

Throwing back the covers, I quickly take stock of my situation. I seem to be modestly dressed in someone else's clothes. My wedding dress is gone, and so are my under garments. Another horrifying thought occurs to me. What if Vinnie caught up with me, drugged my drink and now I'm being held here against my will?

I stick my hand in the waistband of the shorts and

find my panties are still intact. Well, as intact as a lacy white thong can be. I breathe a sigh of relief. Things could be so much worse.

Cautiously, I look around the room. Nothing here looks familiar. It's as if I've been transported back a few generations. I see handmade quilts and there are even candles on the table.

I reach down to grab my phone and realize my garter belt is gone. The panic rises again. What do I do without my phone? I need to tell my family I'm okay — at least I think I'm okay. Honestly, I remember little after I stormed out of the church and hopped into a taxi.

"Oh, man! What did I do after I got into the taxi?" I mutter to myself. Little shards of thought come together as I remember singing to a jukebox in some bar. Oh, yes … Jack Daniels — *lots* of Jack Daniels, which would explain why my head is exploding and my mouth feels like something died in it.

None of those memories account for why I'm here in this strange place and why my clothes are gone. Maybe it's because I am a police officer, but my thoughts can't help but go to some very dark places.

Frantically, I look around for a telephone. My eyes light on the nightstand. To my relief, my phone is sitting there next to my neatly folded undergarments. Alongside, are a container of water, a bottle of aspirin and a package of Alka-Seltzer. This isn't adding up. Maybe Cody came and rescued me again, I don't know. When I grab the bottled water, I notice there is a note under it.

I gingerly lean over to pick up the note.

In a neat, masculine scrawl, the note reads,

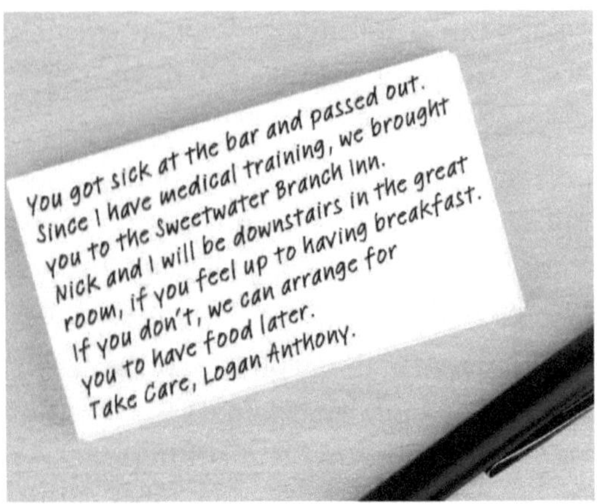

As I study the note, more flashes of last night appear in my consciousness — two first names. I remember two first names. They were attached to a ruggedly handsome guy with kind eyes. I don't usually go for the scruffy type, but then again, my taste in guys seems to be a little suspect.

The other guy was Nick Anderson ... no, that's not right. Weston — like Wesson oil — that's it. He reminds me of my partner Cody. He fancies himself to be a real ladies man. I thought he was cute, but his type is not my thing.

I reach over and grab my phone. There are like ten dozen calls from my parents and brother.

I might as well start with John. He'll probably be more understanding than my parents. He has gotten himself into a few scrapes here and there.

John answers on the first ring. "Katie, are you okay? What did you do? Mom is beside herself with grief. She was sure you'd been kidnapped."

I flinch at his words. My mom has had far more than

her fair share of things to worry about during the last few years. It upsets me to know she was freaked out by this experience.

"I'm okay. I really am. I'm confused about where I am and how I got here."

John clears his throat. "Well … I know where you are. You're at the Sweetwater in the Carriage Room. You should be safe until you want to leave."

"How do you know this? I don't even know."

"Master Sergeant Anthony called me to let me know what was going on."

"Master Sergeant?" I ask. "I thought he told me he provides security for Aidan O'Brien."

"He does. Tristan and Isaac did some digging for me. Both the guys check out. They had exemplary service records until they were injured."

"I know I was kind of drunk, but they didn't look too injured to me. Are you sure they're not pulling some sort of scam?"

"Katie, you should know better than most someone doesn't have to see your injury for it to be present," John chastises.

Dammit, I hate it when my brother is right. I should know better. "I'm sorry, I'm skeptical about guys since Vinnie turned out to be such a flake. For all I know, he arranged for them to meet me and kidnap me."

"That did *not* happen. These are the good guys. They didn't have to call me and let me know what happened to you. Logan didn't have to update me on your blood pressure and respirations to make sure you didn't suffer from alcohol poisoning — but he did. They don't know me from Adam, so they didn't need to treat me with dignity and respect — but they both did. Everything about these guys indicates they were talented soldiers who were in the wrong place at the wrong time like me."

"So, if Logan is so talented as a medic, why is he chasing a rock star around the country? Why isn't he on an EMT squad somewhere?" I ask with skepticism dripping from every word.

"I don't know, Sis. How did I go from being a world-class helicopter pilot to helping launch software for individuals with disabilities? Life is weird. I didn't give them a full-scale debriefing. I was more worried about you. I'm sure if you ask them, they will tell you the rest of the story. They seem pretty up-front and honest to me."

"Okay, I believe you. I'm just stressed out beyond reason. How did it go at the church after I left? Do I even want to know?"

"Tayanita gave me a play-by-play. Apparently, it was fascinating."

"Part of me doesn't want to know this, but the bigger part of me does — Did Cody end up arresting him?" My voice rises with every syllable. My head quickly starts to pound, so I lower my voice. "This is bad, isn't it? I'm sorry John. I couldn't marry the man. He doesn't respect anything about me."

"Vincent didn't get arrested — at least at first."

I groan. "He'll blame me for this. I know he will. He was off-the-wall crazy yesterday. He's won't listen to logic."

"He did try the blame game. He came back in the sanctuary to try to tell all of us what a horrible human being you were. Well, his mother wasn't having anything to do with that nonsense. She shut him right down. Winnifred told him if he couldn't keep a girlfriend, it was his fault, not yours. She's a little sad though, she was looking forward to having grandchildren from you."

"So weird. She and I never talked about kids. Kind of creepy."

"Mom gave me a cat to serve as a chick magnet so I would produce a few grandchildren, don't you remember? I don't think Winnifred has the corner on creepy."

"Okay, you have a point. Perhaps I'm reading too much into it because I'm looking at it through the filter of yesterday. Vinnie seemed desperate to marry me. I can't figure out why he had to get married all of a sudden. We've been together longer than you and Tayanita. He was fine with not getting married until recently. Without warning, he pushed to get married as quickly as humanly possible."

"Winnifred accidentally provided a few more details during their argument. It seems your Vinnie the Pooh was withholding some rather valuable information from you."

"I knew it! He's already married, right?" My stomach sinks to my toes. I'm feeling nauseous again. I try to breathe through it.

"No, his problem is he isn't married yet. I guess he had until he was thirty years old to get married or the inheritance from his grandfather would be null and void."

"The creep was on a deadline to get married?" I exclaim in surprise. "The depth of his depravity is scaring me."

"I take it this means he didn't tell you either?"

"Not a word. I thought the jerk was truly in love with me. However, as we got closer to the wedding date, it became increasingly clear he was often against me and everything I value. I thought it was because my recovery from the gunshot wound was so rough, but it seems like there might be a whole world of other reasons I didn't even know about."

"It's safe to say your Vinnie-the-Pooh, has many layers. Sadly, not all of them are good."

"I know I'll hate myself for asking, but what did the jerk do to get arrested?" I ask as I practically hold my breath. I have visions of him firebombing the church or something.

"Vincent threatened to do bodily harm to his own mother if she didn't remove the restrictions from the will or trust his dad had set up for him."

"I'm guessing there were multiple people in the audience who felt the need to escort him right out of the church. I can't imagine Cody standing for that — or Gareth for that matter."

"You have no idea." My bother chuckles softly. "Vinnie thought he had a built-in fan club — you know, friends of friends who are from the business world."

"Yeah, his family is pretty well connected."

"When they applauded for you and booed him, he nearly had a psychotic break. The very last straw was when he looked right at Ketki and called her a retard. Then the whole crowd turned against him and the police were brought in to establish order. Obviously, since the threats were caught on tape, he can't deny them. So, it should be a relatively quick journey from security expert to convicted felon."

"Watch your back; he's not exactly stable these days."

"I am aware. He has been blowing up my phone with nasty-grams."

"What should I do about this? I'm scared to go home," I ask as I try to catch my breath. I knew it would be bad, but it might even be worse than I anticipated.

John makes a soothing noise. "Please try not to worry. You'll be okay. Master Sergeant Anthony has assured me your room is paid for — for as long as you need it."

"No!" I protest. "I just met these guys. They are not responsible for my well-being."

"Katie, I think you should take them up on it. Your former fiancé is kinda like one of those agricultural systems that spouts poop. Everything out of his mouth is gross."

"Thanks, I'll never be able to un-see that visual. You don't want to know what images are seared in my brain."

"What I can imagine is bad enough," he jokes and then turns somber. "Seriously, stay there where no one can locate you and there are some extra eyes on you. I heard Vinnie yelling yesterday, he sounds deranged. The man doesn't have much to live for or much to lose, which is radically dangerous for you."

"You do realize your advice is all kinds of upside down and backwards. You shouldn't be encouraging me to stay with guys I only met a few hours ago," I argue.

"Desperate times call for desperate measures," John says philosophically.

"How did I get it so wrong? I thought I had learned all the important lessons from my big brother. So, where did I mess up?"

"I don't know, Katie. This conversation is like déjà vu for me. The woman I married originally was someone completely different from who I thought she was."

"Honestly, I have no idea what happened between you and Josselyn. She was a strange one. I like Tayanita much better."

"Katie, please take me seriously. If these guys are offering you a safe sanctuary, take them up on it. I'm no longer in a position to help protect you. These guys protect big-name people for a living and don't bat an eyelash. If anyone can keep you safe, it's these two guys. Do me a favor and trust them, okay?"

"I'll do my best. I make no promises. It is hard for me to trust anyone. I've been burned too often. I'm tired of being a failure at everything."

"You're not a failure at everything. You're having a crappy few months. There is a difference."

"It's funny, it doesn't feel like it's a temporary thing anymore."

"I have faith in you. You'll find a way above, below, around, over, or through — you always do."

I wish I could believe my brother, but honestly these days I don't know who or what to believe in. I feel shattered in a million pieces.

Chapter Four

Logan

My grandma used to say, "Don't waste time eavesdropping because you'll learn nothing flattering about yourself." I probably should have listened to my grandmother a little more.

What started out as a mission to deliver a breakfast tray to Katelyn, has turned into an unintentional recognizance mission. Apparently, she is on the phone with her big brother. I can hear the speakerphone through the door. I left the door open a crack last night so I could hear if she had any disruption in her breathing. As a result, I can clearly make out both sides of the conversation.

Although it stings to hear her question both my disability and my intentions, I can't say they are not things I've thought about before. To look at me, you would never guess I live with the effects of getting shot every day. I look totally normal, yet I am not fit for service in the military. It's FUBAR at its finest.

After Katelyn signs off with her brother, I balance the tray in one hand while I knock on the door with the other.

"Good morning, Sunshine. How are you this morning?"

"Not so loud, please. My brain is threatening to move to a new country, and my stomach isn't far behind."

"I brought you some stuff to help you."

"Eggs and toast?" She lifts the dome examines the plate in front of her. "This was sweet of you, but I don't know if I can handle this today."

"I brought you some ginger ale to help settle your stomach."

"Thanks, I appreciate it. I'm not sure ginger ale can cure what's wrong with me. My humiliation levels are off the charts. I don't usually do what I did last night. I'm not a sloppy drunk, I swear."

"I never thought you were. Sometimes, life catches up with us and kicks us in the butt. You do the best you can to cope. So, if that means getting sloshed at the bar, more power to you."

"I see like one-and-a-half of you this morning, but where is the other guy? You know … the flirt."

"He got called away because one of our principles left her meeting and needs to go across town to a different recording studio."

"Oh, right. Tasha Keeley is touring with you guys. I bet you have a hard time with crowd control around her. She's beautiful."

"Her fans are different from Aidan's for sure."

I take a few moments to look her over. She looks a little pale, but her breathing is better.

Katelyn shivers, and her teeth chatter as she tries to talk. "I don't know what's wrong with me, but I'm so cold."

"Let me grab my medical kit, and I'll check it out. I think it's because you had a lot to drink last night. You are pretty small, and you were putting it away like someone who weighs twice as much."

"Last night was not my finest example of decision-making. It would be ridiculous for me to claim otherwise — as evidenced by the fact I woke up in a stranger's bed and I don't remember how I got here," she answers. "Maybe I should swear off Jack Daniels for a while."

"It's pretty brutal and can do a number on a lot of people. I'll get my kit. I'll be right back to check everything out."

Katie's eyes go wide. "So, you're telling me you want me to agree to play a grown-up game of 'Doctor' with you?"

I smirk, "Although that would be fun, it's not the type of medical care I'm providing today. I was planning to take your blood pressure and run a glucose panel on you."

"Oh wow! You are serious. You happen to carry all that stuff in your ready kit? That's the definition of prepared."

"I am very good at my job. Some of my gear is personal though. I can't leave my house without my glucose meter, compliments of Uncle Sam."

Between chattering teeth, she asks, "What do you mean?"

"I'll be right back. I'll tell you about it once I've taken your vitals."

Fortunately, I put the medical kit right in front of my door in case I had to render aid last night.

As I enter her bedroom, I place the stethoscope around my neck and dig out my glucose meter. I take a moment to change the needle and put a new strip in the glucometer.

She watches my actions with trepidation written all over her face.

"You're going to poke me, aren't you? Will it hurt?" Katelyn asks as panic enters her voice.

I shrug. "No, not much. Then again, I might be used to it. The pads of your fingers might be a little tender."

"They are! I've been trying to figure out what I did to my fingers. Did you watch over me all last night? Were you running tests to make sure I was okay? Bizarre — I'm a perfect stranger to you — why would you bother?"

"Because it was the right thing to do," I respond succinctly. All this praise makes me want to twitch. I like to be in the background and invisible.

"I guess I picked the right people to pass out in front of. Someone else might have done something violent to me in the back alley behind the bar. Score one for being a great human being."

"Like I told the bartender, I have sisters, and I would want someone to treat them with kindness and respect."

"I'm not sure poking me with a sharp object counts as kindness and respect," she teases.

"It is if you're at risk for blood alcohol poisoning. You were really out of it last night. I'll admit, you made me shake in my boots a little. It's been a while since I've done any rescue work."

"Did I mention I am afraid of needles?" She shudders.

"A lot of people are, but you don't need to worry — this meter has a teeny tiny needle. You won't even notice it. I do this between five and seven times every single day."

"Good grief! Why would you want to torture yourself?"

"I don't want to. Still, I have to … since a bullet took out a large piece of my pancreas. I'm now diabetic."

"Really?" she blurts in surprise. "I'm sorry, that was inappropriate, but I can't get over how fit and active you look. I guess I associate diabetes with older age or little kids. I never considered what would happen to the folks in the middle."

"We have to learn to manage our disease, like any other person with diabetes. The only difference is mine was caused by a bullet. It was sudden and dramatic, and a trauma all of its own — aside from the recovery from an almost lethal bullet wound."

Katelyn grimaces. "Something I relate to all too well. I could go forever without getting shot again. It is not an experience I want to repeat. I'm still not back to one hundred percent."

"Do you have any permanent damage?" I ask.

To my surprise, Katelyn throws back the covers and rolls up my T-shirt. She twists her torso around so I can see her wounds.

I whistle softly. "Quite a price to pay for not wearing your vest."

Katelyn shakes her head, grabs it, and moans in pain. When she can catch her breath, she responds, "Remind me never to drink JD again. Anyway, would you believe I was wearing my vest? The bullet found a tiny gap under my arm and made it in."

"Oh man! That sucks!"

"Yeah, most of my damage was internal. It nicked an artery to my heart and broke several ribs. If Cody hadn't been there to stop the bleeding, we wouldn't be having this conversation."

"I bet rehab was rough," I commiserate.

"Yeah, I had nerve damage in my shoulder under my scapula. It slows down my shooting. Something about the body mechanics is off. It doesn't seem to make any difference how much physical therapy I do, I'm not back to where I was before. It ticks me off too. I was one of the best shooters in the Academy."

"How long has it been? I know my rehab seemed to take forever."

"Too darn long. I've been riding a desk for almost a year and a half."

"That's a while. I'm sorry."

"Me, too. I think I'm being punished for being involved in and officer involved shooting. I know my supervisor would just as soon fire me, but we got so much publicity from the shooting he doesn't dare."

"What an awkward position to be in," I remark. "I don't envy you at all."

"Yeah, it's ba —" she mumbles, slurring her speech slightly.

Katelyn slumps back against the pillows as if the conversation took everything she had.

The abrupt change in her presentation snaps me into full-on professional mode.

"I'm sorry, Katie. This will sting a little, but I need to do it," I say as I use an alcohol prep pad to clean her finger off.

"Been shot. Can handle this. Not a baby," she mutters.

"Never said you were," I place one of the testing strips in my machine and poke the side of her finger. I collect blood on the small strip.

When I see the number pop up on the LED screen, my eyes widen. "Katelyn, when was the last time you ate something? Your blood sugar is low — dangerously low."

"I don't know. I think I ate a few crackers to settle my stomach before the wedding. I was massively nervous and distracted. Honestly, it slipped my mind."

I walk over to my backpack, which is sitting next to my medical kit and take out a couple of glucose tablets. "Take these. They will make you feel better."

"I'm almost as bad about taking medicine as I am at getting shots. Do these taste awful?"

I shrug. "They taste like candy to me."

She opens her mouth like a little baby bird, and I pop them in. As she starts to suck on them, she says, "They're a bit like Tang."

I nod as I consider her statement. "It's been a long time since I've had any Tang, but I suppose you're right. How are you feeling?" I ask after a few moments.

"A little less shaky."

I lift the lid on her breakfast tray. "You need to eat something else with protein in it."

As soon as she sees the food, she sits straight up in bed and declares, "I need to go to the bathroom."

I scoop her up from the middle of the bed and quickly stalk to the bathroom door. "Do you need some help?"

She gags as she shakes her head.

"Are you sure? I used to be a field medic. I've seen about everything there is to see."

"No! Let me be miserable in peace, okay? I did this to myself — you don't need to pay the price for what I did."

I'm not sure she remembers throwing up next to me twice last night. I'm not about to remind her. She's already beating herself up enough as it is. My stomach rebels slightly as I hear her wretch several times. Even all the time I spent in the field didn't cure me of my gag reflex.

Finally, after several minutes, I hear her flush the toilet and turn the water on in the sink. "Are these toothbrushes new?" Katelyn asks through the door.

"Yeah, the bed-and-breakfast provided them for us."

"Mind if I use one?"

"Knock yourself out. If you want, you can take a shower, but I think if I were you, I would sit down on the ledge."

"I would love to take a shower and wash the beer smell out of my hair, but I don't have any clean clothes. By the way, what happened to my wedding dress?"

"The proprietor of the Sweetwater has a tall coat closet that accommodates your dress perfectly. I didn't want it to get ruined."

"It's probably far too late, I literally stuffed myself into a taxi and went to the bar. Who knows how dirty it is? On second thought, it probably doesn't matter because I'm never wearing it again. One traumatic experience is enough."

"You can go ahead and enjoy your shower. I have clothes here for you."

"How in the world do you have clothes for me?"

"It turns out we have a really talented wardrobe person. Bianca is the best. She dropped some clothes off for me. Knowing her, they are probably the perfect size. She's good even if she doesn't see our stars in advance."

"Talk about going above and beyond the call of duty. You did not have to get clothes for me."

"It wasn't any big deal. I'm sure Bianca had fun shopping for a new person."

"You bought me *new* clothes? They're not from a thrift store or something? Crazy."

"No, I don't think it is. Once Nick and I learned about the circumstances surrounding your little field trip to the bar, we decided it might be safer for you to stay in for a while."

I hear her growl in frustration. "You guys can't decide when I can come and go or where I can be seen. What made you think you have the right? I am a fully trained police officer. I can handle this stuff."

I sigh as I rest my forehead against the bathroom door. "I know you don't remember much about last night, but you were not in any position to handle anything. So, Nick and I did a threat assessment based on what you told us and the other people at the bar. If it has changed now that you're thinking more clearly, we can talk about it."

For a couple minutes, all I hear are the sounds of her

brushing her teeth. There isn't a lot I can do other than wait. She has to process all of this on her own.

Finally, the door opens a crack, and I can see she's been crying. I grab a paper towel off the top of the microwave and hand it back to her. She wipes her tears and says solemnly, "For reasons you might expect, I don't feel well enough to fight about this yet. You're right, a shower does sound good to me. If you don't mind, I'll take those clothes you so generously bought for me. Maybe cleaning myself up will help me get my head on straight."

"You've had a rough twenty-four hours, don't worry about it. That's what I'm here for."

"Logan, you know I can't afford your services. Since they have me on desk duty, I'm not getting any overtime. I can barely afford my mortgage. I don't even want to think about all the expenses for the canceled wedding."

"Who said I was charging you? Right now, I am on vacation and my time is my own. I can choose to use it how I wish. It's worth it to me to prove to you not all guys are like Vinnie the Pooh."

Chapter Five

Katie

I stand under the hottest shower I can tolerate and lather up my hair for the third time. I let the water run down my back and over my torso as I contemplate how to recover from last night.

Logan is right. I did lump him in with Vincent. It's probably wrong of me to do because he has shown nothing but kindness and tolerance despite my crazy behavior last night and this morning. Even so, part of me can't help but be skeptical. I remember Vincent was attentive and kind in the beginning too. What if this is some weird grace period between Logan and me?

Yet, my big brother's words loom large. If I've learned anything in the time John and Tayanita have been together, his employers give a whole new meaning to the words 'thorough background check'. Basically, if Identity Bank has cleared these guys, chances are, they are squeaky clean.

After I was shot, Isaac Roguen practically adopted me. He used to bring me little treats his wife made and he would sneak designer coffee into the hospital for me. When I tried to pay him back for his help, he told me he owed it to me one law enforcement officer to another. It was one of the nicest things anyone has ever done for me. With very few exceptions, my colleagues generally look down on me as if I am somehow weak and incapable. I don't know how much of it is my gender, or my size or the fact I'm green. After all, it wasn't long ago I graduated from the police academy.

Isaac's respect is a welcome change from my usual workplace. I have a feeling if I can put aside the chips on my shoulders from my past, Nick and Logan might look at me with the same amount of respect.

I shouldn't have jumped down Logan's throat for trying to keep me safe. He's right. Last night I was incapable of making rational decisions or protecting myself. It isn't fair to hold the man's job against him. It's not any different from people having all sorts of stereotypes and assumptions about me as a policewoman.

I unwrap the soap and begin to soap up my body when I feel the remnants of my scar. Even after a year and a half, the scar is raised and angry. It's like my whole body is rejecting the fact there once was a bullet inside of me.

I step out of the shower and wrap a towel around myself. When I walk past the mirror, I practically jump in surprise. I don't even recognize myself. I look hollow. It's as if I've lost my spark. I thought I was getting it back, and then Vinnie-the-Pooh happened. I still don't know how I got in so deep. If I put on my police officers hat and take off the hat of the person who thought she was deeply in love, I can admit to myself Vincent had a way of gas-lighting me — he tried to alter my reality by telling me something else happened or dismissing the way I felt about everything — from what we ate for dinner to whether we would get a pet. If I had known from the beginning what kind a person Vincent was, I would have run the other way. Unfortunately, I didn't because it all seemed so perfect and comfortable.

Logan's words are like a splash of ice water in my face. He is talking as if I'm in eminent danger. I suppose I should pay attention. Still, I have a hard time envisioning Vincent, the square bookish type who likes to crack intellectual jokes about things like chess and water-polo, as a real threat. Of course, I'll probably be proven wrong a thousand different ways. I guess it's hard for me to give up my dream of having the kind of marriage my parents have. If I step back, I know that dream was never obtainable with Vincent. He doesn't have enough empathy and compassion for my taste.

Still, does all of this rise to the point where we need to call it a "threat assessment"? Seems overly dramatic to me.

I jump when I hear a soft knock at the bathroom door. I open it a crack and peek out. Logan wordlessly hands me a large garment bag filled with clothes. "Thank you, this is so much better than wandering around in a beach towel," I comment with a smile.

When I pull the beautiful items out one by one, I realize they are an exclusive brand I could never afford on my own. As I catch a glimpse of myself in the steamy mirror, I whisper, "Help me!" I don't know how to survive this all. I have a feeling I'm about to enter a whole new world.

As I walk into Logan's suite, I can't resist giving a twirl.

I've never felt so elegant in my life. The crisp linen pants and jacket paired with a silk halter top make me feel like I'm some sort of fashion model.

"What do you think?" I ask cheekily as I give one more slow turn like a model.

When Logan looks up from his paperwork, he grins slowly with a look of unadulterated male interest. His hot gaze is much more appealing than it should be under the circumstances.

"I like it. I like it a lot. You look like you are feeling much better."

"I don't know if I would go as far as saying much better, but I'm a little better, and at least now I'm clean and I smell good."

"I think you look phenomenal. I would hire you any day of the week. You'd fit right in at Silent Beats."

"Really? It would be nice if you weren't joking. Desk duty is not what I had in mind when I signed up for the police academy. I wanted to make a difference in people's lives. Right now, all I'm doing is entering data into the computer. I don't even use my training."

"It's too bad this is Florida, and Silent Beats is headquartered in Oregon."

"Oh my Gosh! I didn't hallucinate that weird call, did I? I actually talked to Aidan O'Brien when I was drunk off my butt. He must think I'm a total fool." I pause for a moment while I collect my thoughts. "Do you mind if I ask you a question?" I ask tentatively.

Logan raises his eyebrow and says, "Be my guest."

"I don't watch all those celebrity shows and stuff, but my mom does. I am curious about whether Aidan and his wife are as nice as they seem on TV. Tara seems like she's pretty much perfect. She's everything a klutzy woman like me aspires to be."

"Tara would probably be pleased to hear that, after she got over her embarrassment. She doesn't like to be told how graceful and beautiful she is. In answer to your question, they are that nice. They are the best employers I've ever worked for, hands down."

I sigh wistfully. "They must be great to work for. Between getting shot and being chained to my desk, I'm seriously second-guessing my career choices."

"I can't say I blame you. I would be too," Logan responds with a sympathetic smile.

I sit down at the table with Logan and look longingly at his coffee.

He pushes it toward me "Would you like some? I haven't touched this cup yet. Be forewarned though, it's pretty strong and totally black. Everyone at work teases me about my affinity for black as tar coffee."

"We are totally kindred spirits. Why mess up a good cup of coffee with sugar and foofy stuff?"

"Exactly! Why water down the glory of the coffee bean? After all, you're drinking it for the caffeine anyway, right?"

"Totally! I wouldn't have been able to make it through the police academy without coffee."

I take a sip of coffee and moan in appreciation. "You are the first person I have ever run across to make your coffee the same way I do. So bizarre."

Logan tilts his head at me. "Glad to be of service."

"Speaking of service, I guess I should be honest with

you and tell you my discomfort with my job probably goes deeper than being shot and put on desk duty."

"Yeah? How so?"

"As a kid growing up, I was always an adventurous, 'go by the seat of my pants and rely on my instincts kind of kid'. I always wanted to be in the middle of the action. I drove my mother absolutely crazy."

"We adrenaline junkies are hard on our parents," Logan comments.

"You have no idea! My brother John used to fly helicopters in the Coast Guard. During the investigation of his accident, I changed my major from sociology to criminal justice. I wanted to be a police officer who made a difference in someone's life. You know, standing on the side of truth and justice everywhere and all that jazz."

"Let me guess — real life intervened, and you lost a few of the stars in your eyes?"

"Big time. When I was growing up, I always thought of police officers as the heroes. I was proud to be part of a fraternity of helpers. After I graduated from the police academy, I learned criminals are not the only people who dislike police officers. In fact, the people I arrest are often nicer than the public in general."

"Really?" Logan asks with surprise in his voice.

"Absolutely. Before I was injured, I was a beat cop. People on the streets were my biggest cheerleaders. Sometimes, I would have to turn around and arrest them for drug charges, shoplifting, prostitution or any number of other crimes. Even so, they never lost faith in me."

"It must be hard to arrest people you consider your friends."

I shrug. "Sometimes. Other times you know they're better off in jail. I had one kid who I knew was being abused at home, but we couldn't gather enough evidence to make the case stick. Every time we thought we had it pinned down, he would recant and put everything in question in his case, I knew he was probably safer in our facilities than he was at home."

Logan grimaces. "No wonder you're feeling burned out."

"Honestly, dealing with the public isn't the most difficult part of my job. It's my coworkers and lack of support from management. There is one guy who completely resents my presence there. When I pass him in the hall, he says, 'A. A.' under his breath. He is convinced it wasn't my sharpshooting skills or how well I did at the Academy that got me the job. He thinks I was hired only because I'm a woman and used affirmative-action programs. I'm so sick of his garbage. How qualified do I need to be to hold my weight among the men I work with?"

"I saw that in the military too. A lot of my female colleagues could out bandage or shoot me. The women were phenomenal at their jobs, but they were never quite given the same respect as the men in the unit. Even male soldiers who were not as qualified were often promoted faster. It pisses me off."

"Thanks for being honest about th —" I answer, but I'm interrupted by my cell phone. "One second. I need to grab this. It's my brother."

John sounds frantic as he barks into the phone, "Tell me you're still there with Staff Sergeant Anthony."

"Yeah, he's sitting right across from me. Why?"

"Katie, listen. You need to put me on speaker phone."

"Uh … okay. Are you okay?" I ask, concerned about the tone of his voice. I push the button for the speakerphone and set my cell phone on the table.

"I'm better now I know you are nowhere near your car," John answers emphatically.

"Of course I'm not by my car. I left it back at the church. It's in the church parking lot."

"Well, what's left of it is," John says with a sigh.

"What in the world are you talking about?" I ask.

"Somebody firebombed it today. I'll give you one guess as to who I think it is. Of course, not a soul can prove anything."

"What about the church's surveillance camera?" I ask as feelings of dread push up from my stomach.

"It turns out the one covering the back corner of the lot was a dummy camera."

"I hate it when they do that! It ties the hands of the police. Surveillance cameras are inexpensive."

"I think you're missing the headline here, Sis. Your car looks like our barbecue did after dad set it up wrong."

"Shoot! I just got a new car. Why does all this crap happen to me?" I exclaim. "I don't even know if my insurance will cover my car being turned into one large s'more."

"I'm sure they will, and if they don't, I've got you covered. Your car is not what I'm worried about. I'm afraid for you. If Vincent would do this to random property, who knows what he'll do to you. You need to disappear for a while."

"Who is investigating this? Please tell me it's Cody," I plead.

I hear a long pause on my phone before my brother says, "I wish I could. But you know he can't be in charge of the investigation because he had interactions with the perp."

"Crap! You're right. Watch, it'll be just my luck — I'll probably draw the short end of the straw and get assigned to Milton."

"Got it in one," John says somberly.

"Are you serious? Are you trying to tell me my whole career as a police officer is being held in the hands of a guy who wouldn't know how to find a new car at a car lot?"

"I hate to be the bearer of bad news, but a guy by the name of Harvey Milton in charge of your case. I have his business card right here. Is it as catastrophic as I think it is?"

For a moment, I lay my head down on the table as I say, "It's the worst kind of news. We might as well give up trying to figure out what happened. I don't know if I even want the case to go forward if Milton is at the helm. I can't stand the thought of him pawing through my life."

"No, that's unacceptable. You need someone to look into this. You are in real danger. I feel it in my gut."

"John —" I protest.

"No, Katie, stop. This isn't something you can charm me out of. Who knows what would've happened if you would've been around your car when he lit it on fire?"

"I don't know, Johnny. If Vinnie did this, where can I hide? He knows every second of my schedule." I wipe tears from my face as I toss my phone toward Logan. "You talk to John. I have to go throw up."

CHAPTER SIX

LOGAN

THAT'S ONE OF THE most difficult conversations I've had in a long time. The guy clearly loves his sister. I know what it's like to not be able to protect the ones you love. Even so, I don't know how I can help him. Aidan's tour is wrapping up and we're headed back to Oregon soon. As much as I want to help, I'm afraid my hands might be tied.

On a whim, I pick up my phone and call Aidan. The man is going to think I'm totally insane. "Hello?" Aidan says gruffly. "I hope this is important Logan. Tara and I don't have much time together, and you are interrupting it — if you know what I mean."

I'll be darned if I'm not blushing at his frank admission. "Okay, I won't keep you long. I just want you to know I may do something highly unorthodox, but I need you to trust me."

"Logan, we go back so far it's not funny. So, if you feel you need to do something, you have my blessing. Now if you'll excuse me, I have other plans for my day."

"Don't do anything I wouldn't do," I joke.

"You better not even be thinking about doing what

I'm about to do with my wife. I am generous to a fault, but I draw a hard line at sharing Tara."

"Don't sweat it, I'm not doing that with anybody right now and I would never do it with Tara."

"Listen, it was a joke. I know you would never be dishonorable," Aidan says.

"The same goes for me. I was razzing you — about Tara, not about the other thing. I'll explain more when I see you tomorrow afternoon for practice. I should have a better handle on it by then."

"I trust you with my life — quite literally. Feel free to do whatever it is you need to do."

"Thanks, Boss. I appreciate it."

"Don't mention it."

I click the end button on my phone and stick it into my pocket. It went much smoother than I expected. Then again, he doesn't know what I have in mind. I wasn't kidding when I told Katelyn he is one of the best supervisors I've ever worked for. I can be completely autonomous with him and he never questions my judgment.

Even though my conversation with Aidan went well, it doesn't guarantee Katelyn will be as amenable. I'm not sure she fully appreciates how dangerous it is to leave someone who wants that much control. John is very concerned, and he does not strike me as a man prone to hysteria. I have dealt with hysterical family members before. My hunch tells me he is not one of them. I don't know how she got mixed up with the likes of Vinnie, but it might take some delicate extradition to keep her safe.

My watch beeps to remind me I need to check my blood sugar. When I look at the time, I'm shocked. John and I talked longer than I anticipated. I grab my medical bag and walk next door to check on Katelyn.

Her door is partially ajar, but I knock anyway. I hear her answer, but it's garbled, so I enter the room cautiously. Instinctively, I reach for my waistband. I forgot I left my sidearm in the lockbox on the bus.

I'm alarmed when I find Katelyn sitting in the middle of her bed hugging her knees with big tears rolling down her face.

"Are you all right? Are you feeling ill again?" I ask as I dig through my medical pack for my stethoscope.

"You can put that away. I'm not sick; I'm heartsick. To tell you the truth, I'm heartsick and righteously hung over. It is not a great combination, let me tell you."

My phone alarm sounds off again. Irritated, I swipe at it to shut it off. "Crap, I thought I turned this thing off. I must've hit the snooze button."

"Are you late for something?" Katelyn asks.

"A little. I was supposed to check my blood sugar about ten minutes ago," I explain as I grab my bag. "If you'll excuse me, I'll be right back."

"You don't have to go anywhere. I am good with other people getting jabbed with a needle. It's only a problem when I'm the one getting stuck."

I shrug. "Okay. I guess I don't have a problem with that. I'm not sure I've ever intentionally tested in front of someone else before. Well, not after they taught me how to collect blood and use the meter properly, at any rate."

Katelyn's eyes widen in horror. "Oh, I did not mean to be offensive. I didn't know you were so private about it."

"I don't know. I think I'm private about it more from habit than necessity. I didn't want everybody at work up in my business and monitoring what I eat based on what they read on Facebook. It's frustrating. Not everyone knows the diabetic exchange system and what food equivalents are."

Katelyn gives me a watery grin. "Are you subtly telling me I should let you have a cookie if you ask for one?"

"I'm not sure how subtle it was. But yeah, you don't have to be my food police for me. I've been living with this for a while, and I know how to manage my own sugars. I want you to treat me like I'm any other guy you picked up at the bar."

"Technically, I didn't pick you up at the bar. Nick picked me up, which is different."

"Okay, you win this argument on a technicality. Seriously you don't have to be my hall monitor. I know what I'm doing."

"Maybe. But knowing what I know about the severe side effects of diabetes, it will be nearly impossible for me to not worry about you. It's in my DNA. I am a helper person at heart."

"So, you have personal experience with someone who has diabetes?"

"Yeah, my grandma's sister had it from the time she was in elementary school. She couldn't remember life without it. Eventually, hers got so bad they had to start amputating her toes. They were just about to go further and amputate the lower portion of her leg before she died. Her doctor said it was because she had not managed her diabetes carefully enough and her organs shut down."

"Wow, that's rough. I hope I never get to that place. I watch my food intake like a hawk because I want to be healthy. Perhaps it's because it's ingrained in me as a soldier, but I've always been an exercise nut."

Katelyn assesses me. "You must not do power lifts. I hate the bulked-up look of guys who spend more time on their muscles than they do on intellectual pursuits."

"Would it interest you to know I have an ongoing subscription to *National Geographic* and *Scientific America*?"

"Well, I don't know. A lot of it would depend on whether you actually read the articles or just look at the pictures."

I stall as I set out all my testing implements on the little breakfast table into her room. I rub alcohol on my finger and poke it. After I collect the drop of blood and run it through the glucometer, I'm surprised at the results. I expected them to be much more off-kilter given the stress of the last few days.

"Sometimes, I do both," I answer her question as I clean up my testing kit. "I don't have a lot of downtime to read. When I find myself on vacation like now, my magazines are all at my home in Oregon. They don't do me much good."

"Don't keep me in suspense! Do I have to run you to the hospital, or anything?"

I chuckle at her anxious response. "No, relax my numbers are great especially considering how many hours it's been since I've eaten."

"I'm so sorry. I've kept you away from your meals. Next time that happens, kick me in the butt and tell me the world doesn't revolve around me. I should have been paying more attention to what you need; we're partners."

"I probably won't literally kick you in the butt. I'll remind you sometimes you need to broaden your focus beyond my health issues. I'm a well-rounded guy."

She sighs. "Broad focus? My life is in so many pieces right now I don't even know which one to pick up and work on."

"I have some ideas. Why don't you come back over to my suite? I have some homemade soup I picked up at the deli. It's chicken, and it smells wonderful. I've also got some crackers, and bananas which should help your hangover a bit," I offer.

She looks down at her outfit and says, "Do you mind if I change? This is a linen suit, and I'm way too klutzy to eat soup in a suit. It would be at the dry cleaners for months if you let me eat in it."

"No, make yourself comfortable. I'll go heat it up."

"A word to the wise, when I go comfortable, I go really comfortable. So, if you have anything against wearing athletic gear or yoga pants speak now or forever hold your peace."

I shake my head. "Whatever works for you is fine with me. The God's-honest truth is if I could work in pajamas, I would do it every day of my life. Unfortunately, when I appear with Aidan on the red carpets, they make me wear a monkey suit."

"Wow! Way to name drop there, Logan. Since I've already talked to Aidan, merely mentioning his name doesn't impress me. I already know you do quality work. Otherwise, I'd be puking up my guts in the middle of a seedy bar."

"I often forget what a big celebrity Aidan is. To me, he's just a guy I work for. You'd like him and Tara. As big as they are, they lead a pretty normal life."

"Even though I haven't been around enough famous people to know how, I'm inclined to believe you. Most guys would have tried to introduce me to Aidan to impress me. You know, the whole 'I'm with the band' song and dance."

I grin. "I haven't said I'm above doing that, but the difference is I actually *am* with the band. I can back up my moves."

"Wait? Are you making moves on me? I thought you were impersonating a Jewish grandma. You certainly try to feed me enough and kvetch about nearly everything."

"You're funny! Of course, I worry about everything. It's an occupational hazard. I'll leave making moves on you to Nick."

Katelyn shrugs. "Okay. Suit yourself. I'm not interested in Nick, but whatever."

I groan as I say, "There are so many ways I could interpret that statement. I don't know exactly what you mean."

Katelyn smiles mysteriously before she says, "Okay … this is good. It means I'm not the only person who's totally confused."

"I'm dying to know what you're thinking."

"Well, if you feed me, I might be able to think more clearly," Katelyn retorts with a smile.

"I'll get right on it." I gather up my medical bag and head toward the door.

"I'll be over in a few. I'll go strip off these clothes and shake off my blues."

"Okay," I croak, trying not to let her see how her

words are impacting me "I'll have everything waiting for you when you finish. Come on over to my suite."

"I'm telling you; those are the words of a world-class pickup artist. I'm starting to believe you and Nick have some sort of racket going on," Katelyn says as she shakes her head. "I can't believe I almost fell for this whole song and dance."

"It's not like that," I insist.

Katie pins me with a stare. "You know, I can't change my clothes until you leave, right?"

I put my hands up in a placating manner. "I'm sorry. I didn't mean to give you the wrong impression. My suite is bigger and has more space to spread out." I pause for a moment and then add, "Umm, I guess I'll see you later."

I kick myself in the butt all the way back to my room. I can't believe I sounded so stupid. I was like a junior high school guy hanging out at the lockers trying to stammer my way through asking a girl out. You would think I would have come further.

Part of my problem is I'm not sure how I feel about the whole situation. After all, Nick was the one who started the flirting, and I don't want to stand in his way. On the other hand, Katelyn is getting under my skin. She is sharp and funny and beautiful. I didn't set out to find anybody, yet I'm drawn to her.

This whole situation is such a mess. I didn't plan to talk about how I feel about everything, but I might have to so we can clear the air about the other things I need to discuss with her.

As soon as I see Katelyn again, all my good intentions fly

out the window. I have now seen her gussied up as a bride and looking like a corporate attorney, but this — *this* is my favorite look of all. She simply takes my breath away. I haven't felt this way since I was in high school.

High school seems like a lifetime ago yet it's as fresh in my mind as if I graduated yesterday. My whole life changed. It changed everything about me from the way I relate to people to my career choice.

Katelyn reminds me a lot of Elyssa. They both were driven to succeed and didn't take shortcuts to get there. Unfortunately, Elyssa's journey got cut short. We had planned to spend a lifetime together — whatever that means when you're eighteen years old and headed off to college. I was convinced she was my one and only.

I can replay that night in my head with the clarity of a Blu-ray. Some people insist time heals everything and the sharp edges of my memories will go away. They lie. My ten-year high school reunion is coming up soon, and the thought is soul-crushing. I never thought I'd have to live one day without Elyssa and now it's been almost ten years.

The day started out with so much hope. Elyssa and I had both received acceptance letters to our first choice of colleges. I was planning to go to West Point Military Academy, and she had been admitted to Vassar. We had everything planned and mapped out to a T. We even knew when we would get engaged. Both of our parents were leery about the seriousness of our relationship because we were both so young. However, *we* knew without a doubt we could make it work.

It was the night of our senior party. Elyssa had gone over to her girlfriend's house to get ready and help her pack for the overnight party. We were planning to meet at senior night and essentially make out all night.

We thought it was funny when I pulled up right behind her girlfriend's car on the way to the party. Elyssa was laughing and yelling out her window at me. It's the last happy picture I have of her in my mind.

When Elyssa's girlfriend was in the middle of the intersection, a huge full-size pickup plowed into the side of their little subcompact car. The impact was so great it completely flipped the car. My mind did not want to accept what I had just seen unfold in front of me. Still, I knew what was real because I could smell gasoline.

I slammed my car into park and ran toward the accident. I had been taught first aid as part of my ROTC training in high school. It was meant to help prepare me for West Point. What it didn't prepare me for was to see my girlfriend with a piece of plastic from the air bag embedded in her neck.

I begged and pleaded with God. I promised to spend my life helping other people if only Elyssa would live.

She did live — for four and a half more weeks. In the end, the neck injury didn't get her, pneumonia did. She had lost too much blood and been through too much trauma to fight the raging infection.

By the time it was all said and done, and I had buried the love of my life, I no longer wanted to go to school at West Point. Fortunately for me, my commanding officer and the ROTC intervened. Lieutenant Commander Leroy Bevins saved my life. He helped me turn my grief into a career plan so I could move forward. Without him, I don't know where I would've ended up.

I was so frustrated by my inability to help Elyssa that I went back and took every first aid class I could get my hands on. Eventually, I was certified as a volunteer EMT. However, my drive to serve my country was deeply ingrained. I had been in ROTC from the moment I became eligible, and I didn't want to throw it all away. So, Bevins suggested I change my MOS to accommodate my new mindset.

Suddenly, I had a world of responsibilities on my shoulders. I was so much more than a gifted student who had his life all planned out perfectly. Most days, I was still so affected by Elyssa's death I didn't even know which end was up. One thing I did know with one hundred percent certainty was I would never be in a situation where I didn't know enough and couldn't do enough to save someone's life.

I open my eyes and notice Katelyn is examining me intently. She appears pensive as she asks, "Logan, what's wrong? You look like you've seen a ghost."

I allow my gaze to settle over her as I study her from the tips of her toenails with little white polka dots to her halter top that looks like it would be most appropriate for Hawaii. She is both adorable and smoking hot at the same time. It's enough to make my brain short-circuit.

"You look beautiful," I murmur.

She looks around as if I'm speaking to someone else before she finally says, "Thank you."

"You're welcome," I remark.

"When I first came in here, you looked mad and sad at the same time. Is everything okay?"

"It turns out you are right; I was facing down ghosts from my past."

She holds her can of ginger ale up and says, "Here's to slaying ghosts of the past and moving on to the ones haunting us today."

I ponder her statement for a bit before I add, "Sounds like a stellar plan."

Katelyn smiles at me. "Thank you. Occasionally I have flashes of brilliance. The trick is sorting them out from the junk."

CHAPTER SEVEN

KATIE

WHAT STICKS OUT THE most about our impromptu dinner together is Logan's silence. The chicken soup and crackers are delicious, but I don't think that accounts for his suddenly quiet demeanor. Finally, I try to break the ice. "Can you do me a favor?" I ask. "Can you call me Katie? I know it's weird, but the only people to actually call me Katelyn are my employers, my mom when she's mad at me, and Vinnie. I get stressed out when you call me Katelyn. My friends call me Katie. After all we've been through, I think I can count you as my friend."

Logan flashes a quick smile. "Katie it is. I think it might fit you better too — especially considering your style."

I look down at my Hawaiian print halter top and cutoff jeans. "What do you mean? I'm decently dressed. I don't think anything inappropriate is showing."

Logan's eyebrows rise in surprise. "Totally not what I meant. I love the way you're dressed. It shows you are secure in your skin and don't take yourself too seriously. I feel like I would be comfortable hanging out on the beach with you."

"You know, that's one of the nicest compliments I've ever received. Sometimes I feel like I can't ever get the clothes and makeup thing right. I've always been more of a tomboy and less of a girly girl. My fashion sense is not well developed."

"If you're saying you have a lack of fashion sense, bring it on every single day. I think you look beautiful."

"Beautiful might be an exaggeration. I don't even have any makeup on."

"No exaggeration on my part. Like I said, you look stunning."

"Nick may have tried to pick me up, but you have better lines. Kudos to you," I respond with a light chuckle. "You mind if I ask a question? It's kind of personal."

"I think we do personal pretty well. Go ahead."

"I've always wondered how musicians and the people who work for them handle relationships. What do you do when you're gone all the time?"

"I'm fortunate. Aidan owns his own label, Silent Beats, so he has a lot of administrative stuff to do. These days he only goes on three or four big tour trips a year."

"Still — you're a long way away from home. What does your girlfriend think of all this?"

"Well … if I had a girlfriend, I'd hope she would understand the challenges of my job. However, I don't currently have a girlfriend, so I don't have to worry about it."

I feel an inordinate sense of relief at his simple disclosure. Before I can process it, I suddenly have an insatiable appetite for more information. There must be more to the story.

Before I can stop myself, I blurt, "Why?"

"Why what?" Logan asks with a puzzled expression.

"Why don't you have a girlfriend?" I take stock of the person in front of me. "You are handsome, funny and kind. I would expect girls to be falling all over themselves to date you."

"Now it's my turn to blush. I know we said we were putting our pasts behind us, but in order to explain my present and future, I have to explain who I once was."

I take a bite of my chicken soup and slowly eat a cracker. "Sounds intriguing."

"I don't know if it's intriguing, it's just my life."

"Why don't you let me be the judge?"

"Okay, but you can't say I didn't warn you this might not be the most riveting thing you've ever heard in your life."

"Consider me warned. I want to know what led you here to this spot. If it hadn't been for you, I don't know where I would've ended up the other day."

"Well, the eighteen-year-old version of me was very naïve and idealistic. I thought I had everything all figured out. I had met the love of my life when we were fifteen. Elyssa and I were planning to go away to college together and eventually get married. I had visions of a white picket fence and kids playing basketball in the driveway."

"I take it that didn't turn out to be your reality?"

"No, my life has turned out to be quite the opposite of what I expected when I was eighteen."

"What happened?" I pry, feeling his tension rise.

"My girlfriend was killed by a drunk driver right in front of me and I was helpless to stop it from happening."

I draw in a quick surprised breath. "I'm sorry."

"Thank you. The only thing good to come out of it was it completely changed the course of my life. Instead of going into bomb ordinance development, I elected to be a combat medic. I had seen enough killing. I didn't want to add on to it, if you know what I mean."

"I do know what you mean. Being shot at and having to kill the perp has made me second-guess every decision I've made in my whole entire career. Death changes you."

"Exactly. It's made me a lot more cautious about planning for the future and allowing someone to get too close."

"I get it. I'm still having a hard time figuring out how to trust anyone again after what I went through."

"I haven't really tried. First, I threw myself into EMT training and then my military service. I would have been a career officer had it not been for getting caught in the crossfire."

"How long ago was Elyssa killed?"

"It's been almost ten years," he responds. His body language changes and he looks completely destroyed by the thought of all those years they missed together.

"That's hard. Ten years is a long time to be alone."

The side of Logan's mouth quirks up. "Tell me about it. My employer and his wife being the happiest couple I've ever seen doesn't help any. Tasha Keeley, the other musician who tours with us, is blissful in her new relationship with our equipment manager, Jude. Coupledom has broken out like a virus. I feel like the perpetually single guy who can't get a date because he's living in his parent's basement."

"Still better than what I have been doing. I've been serially dating losers. For a while, John was calling it my boyfriend-of-the-month-club. I thought it had all changed when I met Vinnie. He looks so great on paper, and in the beginning, it was awesome, but then after I said, 'yes' to marriage, it all changed. At first, I thought the stress of getting married set him off. I didn't realize he is truly dark and ugly."

"Do you ever wonder why it seems the whole world gets the relationship thing and you don't? I tried one of those online dating services. Once the women figured out what I did for a job, I could never decide whether they were actually interested in me or just wanted an 'in' with my employers. It's an awkward thing, to say the least."

"You should try being a female on one of those sites. I've gotten more pictures of people's crotches than I can count. In my case, once the seemingly decent guys found out I was a police officer, they immediately thought I was too tough and macho to be in a relationship. Even worse, were the people who believed I was just playing dress-up cop and assumed I wasn't effective at my job. I don't know which I hated more. So, I gave up."

Logan shakes his head in dismay. "Well Katie, you and I would certainly qualify for some bizarre reality TV show. We have enough drama in our lives. How do you think we should move on from here?"

I sigh as I respond, "I don't know. I'm still getting over the shock of what happened. At any rate, I only took off a week for my so-called honeymoon. I have to be back to work day after tomorrow. I should go home, grab some uniforms and check on my cat."

"Are you sure it's safe?" Logan asks me.

I roll my shoulder. "I don't know. I'll probably end up giving Cody a head's up so he can provide backup. I don't know what else to do. I can't stop my life because some dude who isn't who he pretends to be is upset because I didn't want to marry him."

"If we were in Oregon, I could call in a bunch of law enforcement folks for you. I got lots of contacts in my community. But here, I'm limited. I don't know many people in Florida. Aidan hires this company called Identity Bank to do all his background checks before he puts someone on the label. Perhaps they know of some resources we could tap into."

"Are you kidding me? The company my brother works for provides services for Aidan O'Brien, and he's said nothing to me? That's it! He's getting bright pink socks in his Christmas stocking this year."

"Cute, but wouldn't he be able to tell and just use a different pair of socks?"

I grin at Logan. "Nope. John is blind. He wouldn't be able to tell until people at work point it out to him."

"Wow! Talk about kicking a guy when he's down," Logan says with a look of utter shock on his face.

"No, you don't understand. This is a long running gag between us. I consider it payback for the April Fools' Day joke he played on me. He and his coworkers memorized this whole skit to help convince me John had regained his sight when somebody hit him over the head with a pool cue. I bought it hook, line, and sinker for a while, because John could identify everything in the room with amazing accuracy. I thought I had been witness to the world's biggest miracle — but I was punked by my big brother."

"You guys don't hold back, do you?" Logan asks with a gust of laughter.

"No, together we're basically one huge pain in the butt for our parents. Lord help them when John and I join forces. We're both a little crazy."

"I didn't know your brother worked for Identity Bank. We never talked about it. He was too worried about you."

"Yeah, he's quite adept at the video game stuff. I thought it would be hard for him, but he is helping Tristan and his company find more accessible ways to do stuff. So, it's a win-win for everyone."

"Video games? I didn't know Tristan was involved in those. I've only interacted with him on the criminal background check stuff."

"The way I understand it, Tristan funds most of the activities of Identity Bank with the profits from the software he developed."

"If we talk to John maybe he could get Tristan to help him round up backup for you when you go back to your place?" Logan suggests.

"John doesn't work on that side of things, but I'm sure Isaac and Tristan would gladly take a request from him. They seem open about that stuff."

"Let's get the short-term stuff squared away before we talk long-term solutions to what's going on."

"Solutions? I don't think I have any solutions for the colossal mess I'm in. I think I have to cope with the day-to-day stuff and hope Vinnie doesn't lose his ever-lovin'-

mind again."

"I'm not sure that is the safest plan of action. If I had my way, you would be coming back to work with me. I'd like to put as many miles between the two of you as we can."

"Nice pipe dream, but seeing as how you — and by extension Aidan — are the only two people I know from Oregon, my job prospects as a police officer aren't great there. Besides, since I got shot, I have developed a bit of a reputation as a troublemaker. Likely no law enforcement agency around will want to take a risk on me after I just got shot and killed a man. My record makes me a bad bet for anyone else."

"My read on the situation differs from yours. I think the fact you were shot and still got your shot off accurately is pretty extraordinary. I would love to have someone like you on my team. It goes to show you have good instincts even when you're under stress. Your kind of talent in law enforcement is critical. I've hired people before who are book smart, but when they're put in the middle of the action, they freeze up. Exactly the opposite of what I need when I'm trying to protect Aidan and his artists on his label."

"Perception is an odd thing. I got a plaque and a ceremony from the City Council honoring me for my bravery. I never felt very heroic after the shooting. I felt bad for the guy's family and all they went through."

"How exactly did you get shot?"

"Would you believe I was serving a warrant for a failure to appear on a domestic violence charge? It wasn't supposed to be dangerous."

"I'm not surprised. Situations involving family are

really complicated. Not long ago, we had a problem in-house which turned out to be a relative of one of our team members. It was probably one of the most heartbreaking scenes I've witnessed in a while."

"I bet it was. So, do you want to contact John or do you want me to?"

"Why don't you get some rest? I will handle things with your brother," Logan offers.

"Sounds good to me, thanks. I'm not sure I'm up to going another round with John. He can be overprotective of me."

I glance back at the large team behind me and consider what a bizarre turn my life has taken. Since when do I need an entire entourage of protection to enter my own house? This is surreal and a bit insane. Not only is Cody backing me up, but Tristan's father-in-law Isaac is right behind, along with one of his protégés from the FBI. Logan is right beside me with a taser gun.

"Crap! I wish my concealed carry permit was valid in Florida. This thing is handy, but if we get into real trouble, I'll miss my gun," Logan comments as we walk up to my front door.

"You are going to feel foolish when I open my door and the only thing we find are the dust bunnies in my closet. This, for lack of a better term, is overkill. I'm just getting some clothes."

"Based on my assessment of your situation after talking with your family and other people who attended the wedding, I don't think we are over prepared. If we are, we'll all go out to lunch and laugh at this."

Cody adds, "You need to listen to the man, Partner. I was at the wedding and interacted with Vinnie. Your guy is a few bobbers shy of a full tackle box, if you know what I mean."

"Why am I the last person to figure this out? Did you all know this?"

"I didn't know the extent of how crazy he is, but he was never my favorite for you," Cody responds.

Exasperated, I demand, "Why didn't any of you say something?"

"At first I tried, but you were so blissfully happy you ignored my hints. Then when it seemed like things were going well, I didn't want to burst your happiness bubble."

"Hints? You mean like the times you told me it was going a little fast? Geez Cody, I thought you were jealous I had finally found somebody. How was I supposed to know you thought the dude was dangerous?"

"To be honest, I began to second-guess my gut instinct. I thought perhaps this job had made me jaded enough I saw danger everywhere. I didn't say anything because I didn't want to make you sad," Cody responds as he draws his weapon.

"Cody, you'll scare the hell out of Snoopy," I caution.

"It's my job to keep you safe. Your cat won't even know this is a gun," he says as he rolls his eyes at me.

"You have a cat named Snoopy? I used to have a dog whose name was Woodstock," Logan remarks in a whisper.

The entourage behind me grows quiet as we approach my front door. I'll be honest, my hands are shaking as I put my key in the lock. I'm sure all this is for nothing, but if it's not, I don't know what I'll be facing.

As I open my front door, I cry out. The first thing I see are my shredded curtains. "Darn it! My mom made those curtains for me," I exclaim.

The next thing I know Logan has me by the waist and is pulling me backward.

"What are you doing?" I protest. "I'm a trained law enforcement officer. I do this crap every day."

"I know you do," he growls in my ear, "but you're not always the target. I'm extraditing you from the situation for your own safety."

With no more warning, he drags me down the sidewalk and stuffs me in the car. He hits the top of the car and issues orders to Nick, "Take her to safety."

"But … I don't want to go. I want to see what happened to my home. I don't even know if Snoopy is okay."

"There are others here who can make an assessment, but you need to go. We don't know if the perp is still in the area waiting for you to come home. Nick, get her out of here," he insists.

I sink back into my seat. "Tell Cody not to break any of my crap. I want pictures of the damage."

"I'll have Cody email them to you as soon as we clear the scene," Logan promises as he brushes the hair out of my eyes and slams the car door.

Nick speeds away from my home and I try to breathe as I try to figure out when exactly I lost complete control of my life.

CHAPTER EIGHT

LOGAN

MY HEART IS POUNDING by the time I convince Katie she needed to evacuate the area. Most of the time, I find it amusing when she digs her heels in and is fiercely stubborn. Unfortunately, today, it cost me valuable time. I sprint back to the house and try to draw my sidearm as I approach the door. I let out an expletive when I encounter the Taser gun instead of my usual Glock.

I draw the Taser and carefully enter the house. As soon as I cross the threshold, Isaac greets me with a grim expression.

"You were 68 Whiskey, correct?" Isaac asks without ceremony.

"Please don't tell me we have casualties other than the drapes —"

"Not human ones. This one is feline. Come on, he stopped breathing."

"I'm not a vet," I feel compelled to remind him.

"Today you are."

"Tell me where." I take off at a dead run toward the voices in the back room.

"You're headed in the right direction," Isaac instructs.

As I enter what is clearly Katie's room, I see Tristan holding a black and white juvenile cat. Cody is attempting to perform CPR.

"How long has he been down?"

"I last noticed his chest moving about thirty seconds ago," Cody says. "How sick do you have to be to do this to a defenseless cat?"

It's then I notice there is a laceration on the cat's flank. I look up at Isaac. "Even if I can resuscitate the cat, it's Sunday; I don't know if we can find a vet who's able to do surgery."

"If you can bring Snoopy back, I'll cover finding a vet."

I hold out my hands and Tristan plants the cat there. He is lifeless. My heart sinks. I don't know if I got any miracles to pull out of thin air today.

"I make no guarantees," I warn as I place my mouth over the kitten's nose and mouth and blow gently.

"You want me to keep up with the chest compressions?"

"I guess it couldn't hurt, as long as you're gentle," I say as I draw a breath.

After what seems like forever, the cat squirms.

"Where are we going?" I ask. I turned to Cody and say, "Grab Katie's bathrobe."

"Follow me," Isaac commands as he hustles us out to his SUV. "You hold the cat, I'll drive."

Much to my surprise, Cody piles in the SUV after us.

When he sees my look of shock, he says, "Katie would want us to save the cat first. She doesn't care about the rest of the stuff. Snoopy is Katie's baby. He helped her get through her recovery. If something happens to him, she'll be destroyed."

After what seems like forever but probably was only about eight minutes, we pull up to a Victorian style house. "We're here," Isaac announces urgently.

I gingerly carry Snoopy inside. His respirations are quick, but they are breathtakingly shallow. His little pink nose is almost white. I'm not a vet, but I recognize the signs of shock.

"Stuart, we are bringing in a level one," Isaac announces to what seems like an empty room. "Sorry, we didn't get a chance to call ahead."

Some guy peeks his head out of a room. He is holding a spatula.

"Dinner's gonna have to wait," he comments under his breath. "What's going on with this one?" he asks as he quickly assesses the cat.

"We don't actually know. Katie is having some trouble with a stalker. She went home to gather some clothes and found her place destroyed and the cat like this," Isaac explains.

"Craptastic. Let me see what I can do. Has he ever lost consciousness?"

"And then some," I respond. "For a little while, he was dead. I did some modified CPR to bring him back to life. I'm not a vet, so it was an extreme stroke of luck," I explain.

The doc grabs a stethoscope off a hook on the wall and listens to Snoopy's chest. "At least you bought me some time. Let's go see what we can do for this little guy. Does anybody know what his name is?" the vet asks.

"His name is Snoopy," Cody answers.

"Clever — one of my other clients has a sister with a cat named Snoopy."

Cody looks up at him in surprise and says, "Oh, you treat Tuffy?"

"Shoot, I was hoping it wasn't the same cat," the vet answers with a tight expression.

He is trying to listen to his chest as we walk. We reach the back room and I set the cat on the operating table. "I don't know what you can do. It seems like he has lost a lot of blood."

"I'll do my best to save him."

I sink down onto a stool. "That's all anybody can do. Let's hope we have a positive outcome."

After Snoopy woke up from anesthesia, Stuart told us it was safe to go home. Apparently, the kitten will take several hours to recover from the effects of the drugs.

As Isaac, Cody and I get into Isaac's SUV, Cody says, "Heck of a thing."

"I know. It's enough to give me nightmares in the freakin' daylight."

"I'm anxious to see what else is back at the house," Cody replies. "I'd bet you my coffee fund it's her ex. I never trusted the guy much. He was too intent on pouring on the charm. Most people who see Katie and me together assume we are a couple. Guys are almost always threatened by me. Yet, Vincent tried his best to make me his best buddy. It was unusual enough to make the hair on the back of my neck stand up."

"You see any other warning signs?"

"Nothing that spelled homicidal maniac. I just thought he was weird. He morphed himself into what he assumed was Katie's perfect guy. He started liking the same foods, movies, and books as she did. I found this especially fishy, considering Katie likes old historical romances. It didn't seem like his genre, but he played right along. If you ask me to name someone who writes historical romances, I couldn't, but somehow he knew her top six or seven favorites."

"I'd find that odd too; we sometimes see it in fan letters. Fans often want to get close to our musicians, so they'll try to replicate all the little quirks and wardrobe choices of our stars."

A chill seems to go up Cody's spine as he says, "Full-fledged creepy."

"It is, but we have enough experience now to spot them a mile away. It's the job of my team and my people to make sure the people who work for Silent Beats are safe."

"As crazy as fans are on the Internet, I can imagine that's your full-time job — plus," Cody comments.

"It is. But I've been with Aidan for several years now, I wouldn't have it any other way."

"Is the house cleared? Is Forensics finished?" I ask. "I don't want to be responsible for contaminating a crime scene. This is going to be hard enough to solve as it is."

"It is my understanding forensics has already

processed the scene," Cody responds as he double checks his messages on his cell phone.

Instinctively, I put on the paper booties sitting outside Katie's door. As Tristan greets the three of us, he places a hand on my shoulder. "Brace yourself; it's pretty brutal in there."

"Anybody injured aside from Snoopy?" I ask, preparing for the worst. I'm barely inside the threshold and already I want to puke.

"Not as far as we can tell," Tristan answers. "It appears he went after the cat with a knife."

As I step inside the foyer, the whole picture becomes clear. I was so focused on getting the cat the first time, I blocked all this out. Whoever this is clearly is trying to obliterate Katie's sense of well-being.

Katie's whole house has been violently tossed. Every cushion, blanket, pillow and piece of artwork has been obliterated.

"Do you think whoever did this was trying to hurt the cat or did the kitten get in the way?" I ask.

"I'm not sure. I don't know how we would prove it without a straight-on confession from whoever this piece of garbage is," Isaac comments.

I turn to Cody. "This is a pretty thorough job. I wonder if it's a professional. Is there anybody in her unit who hates her enough to do this?"

Cody shrugs. "She doesn't share a lot with me. I know some of the old-timers are not truly onboard with having young women on the force. There are a couple of people in our station who think Katie only got the job because she was a woman."

"*¡Dios mío!*" Isaac spits. "Women have been serving with the feds for most of my career. I can't believe in today's world, she still faces gender discrimination." He pauses for a moment and then adds, "On second thought, maybe I can believe it. Some people will never grow up."

"Hold up!" Cody cautions. "Before we start to blame it on a colleague, let's remember she has a crazy ex-fiancé who lost his mind at their wedding. He would be my first suspect — he was bat-flip crazy at the wedding. I think Katie's mom has some of it on video if you need to see more evidence."

"Let's not forget all the suspects she has helped put away," Tristan remarks.

I slowly make my way around the house. When I peek into the bathroom, it's like walking into a scene from a horror movie. I call to the others, "Hey, did you guys see this when you cleared the bathroom?"

Everyone piles into the doorway as if it's a scene from some deranged cartoon scenario. When Cody sees it, he lets out a string of expletives.

"There is simply no question, we must get Katelyn out of here," Isaac announces, "preferably as far as we can get her to go."

"It's too bad I can't take her to Oregon," I remark.

"Why can't you?" Isaac challenges.

"For one thing, we just met last weekend, and I have no claim over her. I have no idea whether she would even consent to a cross-country move."

"I don't know how much weight I carry with her, but I can try to convince her it's a good move. If nothing else, it would work temporarily until we figure out who this maniac is," Cody suggests.

"Thanks, man, I appreciate it. I don't know how much it will help. In case you haven't noticed, your partner is a tad bit stubborn. Even when it comes to her own well-being," I respond as I shake my head.

"A statement like 'You're NEXT!' scrawled in blood on the mirror might work toward persuading her, don't you think?" Tristan asks.

"Like I said, I haven't known her long, but what I have figured out is she has a very strong will of her own and she's not always predictable."

"Well, let's start by calling forensics back in to make sure they caught this. Is there one team we should request?" Isaac instructs as he looks at Cody.

"I'll have to give it some thought. I want to make sure whoever investigates this is giving it their full effort," he replies. "Unfortunately, the way our department works, it's probably whoever is on call."

"Okay, we'll run a parallel investigation as best we can. Try not to touch anything as you take pictures. I think we need to document this as well as we can without disturbing evidence. It seems like it may not be safe to bet on the local PD being impartial and fair."

"There is an evidence technician I trust implicitly. Her name is Desiree," Cody suddenly blurts.

"What are the odds she'll be on call today?" Isaac asks.

"Pretty good, it's a Sunday, and she is at the bottom of the totem pole when it comes to seniority."

"If she's new, does she know what she's doing?" I

challenge.

"Absolutely. She came from a medical background and is very methodical. She used to do lab testing for pharmaceuticals. So, her protocol is spot on," Cody explains.

"Let's call it in and then check on Katie's cat," Tristan says with a shrug.

"I need to check in with Katie too, she's probably sitting on pins and needles waiting for us to respond to her."

"You can count on it. Patience isn't exactly my partner's strong suit," Cody responds with a wide grin.

"Something tells me she needs some patience to get through this."

"Perhaps you should be her distraction," Cody teases.

"I know you're joking, but it doesn't seem like such a bad idea to be her body man," I respond.

"Good luck. I suspect that she hates men right about now. I wouldn't want to be in your shoes," Cody responds with a grimace.

CHAPTER NINE

KATIE

WHEN I WAS UNCEREMONIOUSLY ejected from my own property, I never expected to find myself at John's workplace. Apparently, someone gave him a head's up because it wasn't long before Tayanita and John showed up, complete with a pizza and some soda. John's boss, Tristan, owns this company and the offices are very well appointed, but they still feel like a prison when I want to know what's happening at my place. I restlessly pace some more. Everyone has been gone for what seems like forever.

Tayanita comes into the break room and hands me her phone. "It's the veterinarian who is treating Snoopy. His name is Stuart."

"Hello?" I greet, as my heart beats in my throat. My hands are shaking so violently I'm having a hard time holding the phone.

"Is this Katelyn Ashford?" he confirms.

"Yes," I answer quickly. "How is my cat?"

"Well, Snoopy lost lots of blood and I had to stitch up a laceration on his flank, but he seems to be doing better now. I'd like to keep him overnight for observation and I.V. therapy, but you should be able to take your fur-baby home tomorrow."

"I don't know if I'll have a home to go back to tomorrow or not. The crime scene technicians might still be there."

"Don't worry about it, we'll work with whatever your reality is. If Snoopy has to spend an extra day or two in the hospital, it wouldn't necessarily be a bad thing."

"It might not be for you, but my wallet will feel the pain."

"I don't want you to worry. Snoopy's stay is on the house. You were a victim of crime."

"Thank you so much. Let me give you my number so you can contact me directly," I offer.

"Tayanita already gave it to me, so we're good to go. I'll update you if anything happens. At any rate, I'll call you in the morning to give you a status review."

"Thank you so much for your help. I appreciate it. I know Snoopy can't tell you how grateful he is, but trust me — he loves his life."

"It's not a problem. I'm glad I could help. Talk to you tomorrow," he says as the phone goes dead.

I hand the phone back to Tayanita.

"Good news?" she asks.

Tearfully, I nod. "Yeah, Snoopy will live. I can't believe anyone would be depraved enough to hurt such a sweet kitty. All he wants to do is sit on your lap and give hugs. I mean it — he puts his paws around my neck. It's the cutest thing."

"Speaking of cute, your brother has been doing some spying on your new roommate. He is adorable in a Gentle Ben sort of way."

"I know. He's not my usual type. Maybe that's the point. I've been going for the wrong type of guys for years."

"Do you think he's cute?" my future sister-in-law presses with an expectant look on her face.

"I don't even know why I'm telling you this, but yes, I find him cute. His eyes are fascinating to me. They change color based on his emotion. They are the color of deep, rich honey. His smile — don't get me started. He doesn't let loose with one very often, but when he does, it's like the man is being bathed in sunshine."

"It sounds like you have a crush," Tayanita comments with a wink.

"No! Impossible. I can't have a crush on him, I live in Florida and he lives in Oregon. Furthermore, I just got out of a terrible relationship. I'll have credit card bills for the next three years trying to pay off a wedding I didn't stay for."

"I don't know what to tell you, Katie," Tayanita replies with a shrug. "When love hits, it hits and there is not much you can do about it. Remember, when I fell in love with your brother, he didn't even know my first name yet. These things don't happen on a predictable schedule."

"I understand, but I broke my engagement less than two weeks ago. I can't be on the market for a new guy. It's disgusting and weird," I protest.

"When you went to the bar after you left the

church, did you go there intending to pick up some random guy?"

"No! I went because I wanted to forget what was going on in my life. I wanted to get kick-ass drunk," I admit as I blush a deep shade of red. I don't know Tayanita well, so I don't know what she'll think of my admission.

"Well, there you go. If you fall in love on accident, it's not weird or gross. It's fate. As I always say, there are no real coincidences in the world."

"Even if that were true, Logan lives in a totally different state and in a completely different state of mind than I do. He is the head of the security for a huge star. I am a rookie cop who managed to get herself shot. It's not like we travel in the same circles or anything."

"You could," she suggests.

"I could what?" I ask as I kick my shoes off and tuck my feet under me on the couch.

"People move all the time for relationships or on a whim. If you like this guy, maybe you should follow your heart. I did with your brother and I have never been so happy."

"I don't know if my luck is that good. I would probably end up stranded across the United States with no one to help me and no resources to get back home."

"You won't know unless you try. At least have a discussion with Logan and see if it's something he's on board with — maybe he likes you too."

"Do you realize how insane you sound? Logan is not my boyfriend. We've never even held hands or kissed. Why would he want me to move all the way across the

United States with him?"

"I don't know, maybe it's because you are brilliant, funny, and beautiful," Tayanita answers. She hands me a slice of pizza as she says, "Take your mind off things and eat a piece of pizza. Things will work out the way they're supposed to. I'm sure."

"How can you be so confident? You saw the fiasco of my wedding. Not two years ago or even two months ago — it was two weeks ago. How can I trust my judgment when I fell for a guy like Vincent?"

"One of the things I love about you is how optimistic you are. You always want to believe the best of people even in the face of contradicting evidence. Con artists like Vincent take advantage of people like you. They just do."

"You're saying I'm responsible for this?" I ask with a shocked expression.

Her comment stings more than I would like it to.

Tayanita straightens her back before she explains, "No, that's not what I mean at all. I'm envious of you because you don't have the same level of skepticism about people I do. In the end, I think your optimism will serve you well. This incident is an unfortunate wrinkle in your approach to life."

"How can I make sure I don't fall for someone like Vinnie again? I seem to have perpetually bad taste. Some women go for the bad boys, I go for the psychotic ones," I say with a wry laugh.

"Fortunately, it seems like you have a great one in your sights now," she reasons.

"Logan is one of the good guys, but unfortunately,

he is not mine. After the fiasco of my wedding, I'm not sure I should even think about having a guy in my life — even one as exceptional as Logan."

"I know you're scared. I've been there too. But, you need to ask yourself a question before you decide."

"My life will suddenly make sense if I ask a question?" I repeat skeptically.

"I don't know. I don't have a crystal ball. But, you need to ask yourself if you're prepared to let Logan walk out of your life without giving the relationship a chance to work."

"Okay … but, what if there is no relationship there? What if I move all the way across the country and it turns out to be nothing?"

"John has talked a lot with this guy, and he has a really good sense about him. Think about it. Logan passed your brother's radar. That should say something."

"You're right," I concede. "I can't remember the last time John gave his endorsement to anyone."

"Hey, don't worry. If it doesn't work out, my house is still on the market and I need a tenant in it."

"Does this mean you're rooting for me or against me?" I tease.

"Always *for* you, my dear sister-in-law-to-be. John and I want you to be happy."

"I want to be happy too, but I don't know how right now."

"I understand. If I had gone through what you've been through in the last few days, my head would be spinning too. I'm not telling you to marry the guy tomorrow, I'm just saying you might want to look at your choices involving him."

Five hours, twenty-nine minutes and thirty-five seconds. That's how long it took for Logan to return to the headquarters of Identity Bank. John and Tayanita have been doing their best to keep me entertained and distracted. John even listened to an old movie on the Hallmark Channel based on one of my favorite books. In case I didn't know what a big sacrifice that was for him, he made sure to mention it. Repeatedly.

John showed me the software programs he was working on to make them more accessible to consumers with disabilities. I must say, I am impressed with my big brother. I have always practically worshiped the ground he walked on, but his transition from sighted to visually impaired has been a rough one. It warms my heart to see him doing so well in his new position.

While I'm waiting for Logan to come back, Tayanita's words are tumbling around in my brain. Am I really brave enough to take the risk? My heart has been shattered by my own stupidity. I don't know if I'm strong enough to make a decision like this. Yet, the more I think about it, the better it sounds. It's not like I have a lot holding me here. I mean, I have a family, but there's nothing to say I can't come back and visit.

My job, such as it is now, has been tainted by my officer involved shooting. Internal affairs completely cleared me. They said not only was it justifiable, but it was commendable. Even so, some of my colleagues think I should have acted differently. They don't even try to hide the fact they are giving me the cold shoulder.

Working for Aidan O'Brien sounds like the perfect fix for everything wrong in my life. Still though, I can't help but wonder if Logan really has a position available or if he's just using it as some elaborate flirting device.

As I stew in my own thoughts and try to figure out how to broach the subject with Logan, he comes into the break room and shuts the door. I am alarmed by the grim expression on his face. "Is it Snoopy?" I ask, feeling panicked. "I thought the vet would call me if something changed."

"No, as far as I know, Snoopy is doing really well. I checked in about an hour ago and he is back on his feet. He's taking fluids and resting well. I think your cat may have used up one of his lives, but it seems like he'll make it."

"So, if Snoopy is doing well, why do you look like you are about to tell me catastrophic news?"

"I don't know if it's catastrophic, but it's serious," he responds as he sits down beside me and pulls out his cell phone. "Before you look at these, you need to know they are upsetting. You don't have to look at them if you don't want to. Cody says to tell you that you should buy a lottery ticket."

"Why in the world? I'm not having a streak of good luck. In case no one noticed, my apartment was demolished."

"I guess it depends on your perspective; you weren't in it, fortunately. However, I think Cody was referring to the fact you got both Gareth Tanner and Desiree Bottsworth assigned to your case."

"I wonder how many markers he had to call in to make it happen," I mutter to myself.

"Cody thought you might say that. I'm also supposed to tell you he had nothing to do with the decision. He is steering clear of any of the politics around this — in case Vincent ends up being your perp. I guess he and Vinnie got into it the other day. He wants to stay as neutral as possible — hence he did not call in any favors."

"Cody is a by-the-book kind of guy. Sometimes I appreciate that about him, and other times it's a royal pain in the butt."

"At any rate, your case is being handled by people Cody respects and trusts. So, if you don't want to look at these, there is no reason for you to put yourself through the trauma."

"Trauma? How bad are they?" I ask as my voice rises to a near squeak.

Logan nods solemnly as he explains, "I would be upset if I saw them."

I give myself a mental shake before I say, "I have an annoyingly persistent personality trait. I often act on sheer bravado and hope it's eventually replaced with actual bravery. I want to know what's going on in my home, even if it's awful."

"It *is* pretty awful. You already know Snoopy was attacked. Someone used a knife to cut him. He almost didn't make it because of the blood loss."

I wipe tears from my eyes. "My poor baby. He's such a friendly little cat, I bet he had no idea what was coming."

"Well, whoever hurt Snoopy is a pretty sick psychopath. They sliced up everything in your house from your couches to your bed. They even got your bath towels and your clothes."

"Oh my God! Creepy; they were throughout my whole house. I'm in the middle of painting my closets, so my bath towels are being stored by my pantry in the garage."

"Whoa! Adds a whole new layer of complexity to the situation. Make sure you tell Officer Tanner when you meet with him. It could help him narrow down suspects."

I pin him with a cold stare. "You do remember this is what I do for a living?"

Logan has the good grace to blush. "Sorry, an occupational hazard. I forgot who I was talking to for a moment."

"So, aside from the fact I have to hit a ton of yard sales to replace all the stuff this person destroyed, what makes it so creepy?"

Logan scrolls through his phone. Finally, he pauses to look at a picture. "This is hard. I know you want to see this, but every instinct I have wants to hide it from you," he whispers.

"No fair!" I protest. "I'm more than qualified to look at crime scene pictures. I graduated near the top of my class from the police academy. Forensics was one of my strong suits."

"Katie, I'm not questioning your qualifications as a law enforcement officer. I don't want to show you because I like you and I don't want to see you suffer any needless pain."

"You can't protect me from everything. It's not your job. Despite how you found me the other day, I am a big girl and I can take care of myself," I insist.

Logan exhales before he relents. "Against my better judgment I'll show you. Just know I'm so sorry this happened to you. You might be embarrassed by your behavior at the bar, but in the end, it might have been lifesaving. Your drinking caught Nick's eye before you passed out, which is how you ended up in the safety of the bed-and-breakfast. If you had gone home, it might have been an entirely different story."

"Logan, save the dramatic speeches. You're freaking me out. Show me the picture, please? Let me deal with the facts as they are."

Reluctantly, Logan hands me his phone. Scrawled in big angry letters on my bathroom mirror are the words, "You're NEXT."

A shiver goes up my spine as I ask, "Do I want to know what he used to write with? I don't wear red lipstick and I don't have any catsup in the house."

"The words on the mirror came back positive for feline blood," Logan informs me quietly.

I sway when I consider the ramifications. "Are you sure?" I can't help myself from asking.

"Yes, part of what took us so long is we asked the lab to run it twice."

"So, this is more than a false positive on a presumptive test?"

Logan nods. "Unfortunately, it is likely Snoopy's blood. I don't have to tell you the statistics for comorbidity with people who mutilate animals and move on to human victims. I think you are in grave danger."

"I know I've been downplaying the danger of all of this crap while you've been arguing it was potentially serious this whole time. That ends here. I know psychologically what that sign means. I don't want to put my family at risk. My mom practically had a nervous breakdown when John had his accident and lost his sight. I can't put my parents through another loss."

Logan presses his lips together in a grim line and then opens his mouth to speak. He seems to think better of it and closes his mouth again. After a couple moments of this, he finally says, "I don't want you to think I'm crazy, but I would like you to come to Oregon with me."

I narrow my gaze and directly ask him, "Why?"

"Katie, I swear it's not because Nick and I were hitting on you. We don't have to be in any kind of relationship. This job offer is on the up and up. I would like you to join my force at Silent Beats."

I swear my tongue is somehow possessed as I ask, "What if I want there to be a relationship?" As soon as the words fly out of my mouth, I slam my mouth shut and put my hand over it. "Oh crap! Did I say that out loud?"

Logan chuckles before he says, "I'm not sure what you want the answer to be, but you did say it out loud. Lucky for me, we can have consensual workplace relationships at Silent Beats. It only makes sense because — well, it's like the dating game. Aidan can't have one standard for himself and Tara and something different for the rest of us. So, it's all cool."

"There are so many things to sort out. What about

my job? What about Snoopy? I've got a lease to own option on my house. I have to decide in the next couple of weeks whether I want to keep it or move on."

"So, let me be clear … are you agreeing to move to Oregon?" Logan asks with an astonished expression on his   face. The look on his face is so comical I laugh. "Yes, I think I am."

"I've got two things to say to that," Logan replies. "First, thank God for small miracles and secondly, you'll love Oregon."

"I hope so. I hope I'm not making the second biggest mistake of my life."

"I will do everything in my power to ensure you don't regret your decision to come home with me," Logan says as he gathers me into a warm embrace.

I rest my forehead on his muscular chest as I admit, "It's so easy to believe everything will work out when I'm in your arms."

"Well, then maybe it's where you need to stay."

"Surprisingly, I don't seem to be in a hurry to go anywhere," I whisper in his ear.

CHAPTER TEN

LOGAN

ONCE AGAIN, KATIE HAS surprised the heck out of me. I expected her to be reluctant to see the pictures after I told her what was coming. Yet, she methodically went through all the crime scene pictures and told me about what things were moved and what stayed untouched. If the shoe was on the other foot, I'm not so sure I would be able to be so cool and composed. She is simply phenomenal.

As if her cool professionalism about her own victimization wasn't surprising enough, she volunteered to come to Oregon. I didn't even have to lay the heavy sales pitch on. I guess we both came to the same conclusions about her safety.

I have to tell my boss we've picked up an extra passenger for the trip home. I hesitate to interrupt him. He and Tara have had an exceptionally difficult year and they are keeping to themselves so they can get some much-needed R&R. However, I think this warrants an in-person conversation.

I pick up my cell phone and dial Aidan. "Hey Boss, I hope I'm not interrupting. Do you have a few minutes for me to come to your suite and chat?"

"Sure, Tara fell asleep while she was reading a book and I'm trying to find something decent to watch on television. I've got time to talk to you."

"I'll be right over," I announce.

I am afraid my confession will be all kinds of awkward. Now that Aidan has said yes to the conversation, I have no idea what to say.

It'll be a dicey conversation. Not only because Katie and I are not actually a couple, but also because her choices and the reason she made them is a bit of a mystery. I don't fully understand why she's moving to Oregon. I'm not sure if it's strictly because of her safety concerns or if there's more to it. The more time I spend around Katie, the more I hope there's something more than professional courtesy between the two of us. I wasn't looking to find anybody, but it rocks that I did.

I stand indecisively outside the door to Aidan's suite for several moments before I knock. When he swings the door open, my eyes widen. I thought my room was elegant and well appointed, but it's nothing compared to Aidan and Tara's.

When Aidan sees my look of astonishment, he jokes, "Don't look now, but your face may freeze that way."

"I'm sorry. I don't know if I'll ever get used to this kind of opulence as long as I live. I know you and I have been friends a good long while, but I am still in awe of the lifestyle you lead."

"Don't look at me. If I had my way, we would stay in a yurt somewhere in the middle of the forest. All this stuff boggles my mind too. More often than not, as soon as the managers of the hotel figure out who I am, they automatically upgrade my room. Sometimes, it's not so great. We've had to make huge trade-offs to make this happen."

"I know. I see you guys make those sacrifices every day," I say. I try not to put my nerves on display by pacing as I gather my thoughts.

"Whatever is going on, spit it out," Aidan says with an amused smile. "You're making me look like the calm one here, a concept which would turn the axis of my whole existence on its head."

I make myself sit down in a chair. He's right. I look like a basket case. I'm not sure why this is so hard. Finally, I blurt, "There's no easy way to explain this, but I have a situation going on in my private life which may bleed into my work. Well, I'm hoping it bleeds into my work."

"I can't wait to hear this. Usually, your line between your private life and your work life is rock solid."

"Actually, this is the first time anything like this has ever happened to me. I usually keep my defenses way up, but this time it wasn't effective," I ramble. "Funny, I never expected the line to be completely obliterated, but I think that's what's going on here."

"Does this have anything to do with the bizarre phone call you made a few days ago?"

"It has everything to do with it," I admit as I run my hand through my hair. The move completely derails my train of thought as I add, "I'll never get used to this new shaggy look. I still have to take a double take when I see my reflection."

"I know, it's odd for me too, but when we met with the security assessment folks, they suggested it to help you blend in with the fans when we're on the road."

"I understand, but it's still weird. I haven't had a

beard since I was trying to blend in with the locals in Afghanistan," I explain. "Anyway, as I was saying, my *situation* has a name. Her name is Katelyn Ashford, but she goes by Katie to her friends."

"Funny, Nick mentioned the same name the other day. What's going on?"

"Crap! I forgot to read Nick in on the situation. He's been pretty scarce these last few days."

"Yeah, he's got something going on back at home. Some sort of family drama, including the possibility of him reuniting with his high school sweetheart. I don't know all the details because I heard this secondhand through Tasha, but I guess he was pretty excited about it."

"Good for him. He talks about Cheryl all the time. I hope he can work it out with her. It's actually good news for what's going on with me."

"What are you talking about?" Aidan asks. "How does Nick's personal life impact yours?"

"Normally, they wouldn't intersect much, but we ran into a potential problem the other day when we stopped to get a bite to eat at the pub. Nick decided for Katelyn's own safety, he would intervene."

"Why?"

"As it turns out, Katelyn had just ditched her scum ball fiancé at the altar and was tossing back Jack Daniels like it was sparkling water to numb the pain. You know Nick had a relative who passed away from alcohol poisoning, so he was concerned about her rate of consumption. He started flirting with her to distract her from drinking, but it was too late. She passed out. So, we took her back to the bed-and-breakfast, and I nursed her through the night."

"How gallant of you. Please don't tell me you and Nick are fighting over her."

"As far as I know, we aren't," I answer with a shrug.

"So, how did a random act of kindness become a 'situation'?"

"We discovered Katie's problems are bigger than a devastated bride crying into her bourbon. Her ex-fiancé blindsided her at her wedding and made threats against her. We don't know if it's related, but her car was firebombed, and her apartment was completely ransacked. They went as far as slicing up her cat. I had to give mouth-to-cat resuscitation to save Snoopy. Her partner has met her fiancé and thinks she is at risk."

Aidan's eyebrows go up. "Partner?"

I nod. "Oh, did I forget to tell you? Ms. Katelyn Ashford is a decorated police officer. She recently took out a violent perpetrator while she was under fire."

"Seems impressive."

"You have no idea. Katie was shot in the torso. The fact she could still take out her attacker is a testament to her tenacity and her skills as a shooter."

"Let me see if I have this straight, Nick was flirting with this lady in a bar and you guys decided to swoop in for the rescue. Then, you discovered her problems went far deeper, and now you want to save her from it all? Did I get all of it?"

Unable to stay seated anymore, I get up and pace in front of the large window. "Pretty much. The only part you left out is the part where I'd like to bring her back to Oregon with us and hire her onto my team."

"Are you sure that's a good idea? What if her problems follow her to Oregon?"

"I don't think they will. I think the crimes against Katie have been more about opportunity and proximity than anything else. Cody, her partner on the force, believes it's likely her disgruntled fiancé. He said the guy has a few screws loose."

"Tell me more about bringing her on board at Silent Beats," Aidan instructs.

"We've grown a lot in the last couple of years. Since you now have Joe Summers and Declan as well as Mindy, our resources are stretched pretty thin. We could use some more people on her team. Honestly, we could use as many as three, but at this point, I would settle for one well-trained person. I don't have the time to train a complete greenhorn."

"Let me run it by Tristan at Identity Bank. He should be able to tell us more about your mystery woman."

"Katie is not much of a mystery to Tristan. Her brother works for Identity Bank."

Aidan's eyes widen with surprise. "Wow, quite the coincidence."

"I thought so too, but John doesn't work on the security side of things, he works in software development."

"Have you discussed this idea with Tristan? What does he think of Officer Ashford?"

"Tristan is down with the idea. He knows I'm trying to juggle too many things by myself and having an experienced law enforcement officer on the team will help. Additionally, with Tasha and Mindy playing on the tour, only having male bodyguards puts us behind the eight ball. Sometimes, I need to cover them in places it is awkward for me to be. Having a female officer would be beneficial."

"I trust you to make the right decisions for the whole team. If you think Officer Ashford would be a good match for us, you have my permission to hire her."

"I think she would be a good match. She is smart as a tack and has a great positive approach to life. Although, based on her relationship with her brother, I think you might want to up your practical joking skills. You've let yours get rusty over the past few years," I quip.

"So Katie is a bit of a loose cannon, is she?"

"Only in the best, most exciting ways. She'll make a fun addition to our team."

"You have my permission. Now … how difficult do you expect it to be to persuade her to move across the United States?"

"She is surprisingly amenable to the idea. I think having death threats made against her scrawled in her pet's blood is a pretty powerful motivator."

"Please tell me the folks at Identity Bank are on this case." Aidan shakes his head in dismay.

"Isaac and Tristan are aware of what's going on because they were providing backup when we first discovered Katie's house ransacked. However, I don't know what their ongoing involvement will be. Quite frankly, it isn't my business. A lot of what Identity Bank does is behind-the-scenes and off the grid. I figured it would be better for me not to ask."

"Probably smart. When we were trying to figure out which employee was embezzling funds from me a few years ago, Tristan kept the whole thing under wraps from me until the very end."

"He has a reputation for being very professional and discreet. If he is involved, it will make me feel better. Cody, Katie's partner, is comfortable with the investigative team. Apparently, Katie was lucky enough to get them by random draw."

"Perfect. Sometimes, things align the way they are supposed to," Aidan responds philosophically. "One last question: does Katie understand we are leaving Florida in seventy-two hours, give or take?"

"If she doesn't, I'll spell it out more clearly. Though something tells me, she'll be there with bells on. I don't think we can put enough distance between her and Gainesville at this point." I reach over to shake Aidan's hand. "Thank you so much for understanding."

"No problem. We all go out of our way to do things for people we love."

"I don't know if I'm there yet with Katie," I insist.

"I know that look; I've worn it for nearly a decade. You have the look of a man who has a piece of your heart in the hands of another person."

"I don't really know. I just know there are a lot of pieces of this puzzle we need to put together and it could go in a million different directions."

"For your sake, I hope the pieces get sorted in a positive direction. Being in love is the best thing that's ever happened to me," Aidan declares with a peaceful smile.

CHAPTER ELEVEN

KATIE

"ARE YOU SURE I am dressed okay to meet your parents?" Logan asks. "I haven't done this since I was in high school."

"Relax. As long as you know how to shoot the breeze about fly fishing, and you like good food, you'll do fine," I assure him.

"I'm sure your parents are very friendly people, but I'm not sure they'll be thrilled you're moving clear across the nation with me. How do they feel about musicians in general?"

"Well, my mom has a huge crush on Billy Joel and Elton John. She was over the moon when she got to meet Billy Joel backstage."

"I'm serious, Katie. What do you think they are really going to think about your move?"

I sigh. "I don't know anything for sure, but I expect my mom to cry and my dad to ask you a bunch of questions about how responsible you are."

"Well, it wouldn't be out of the ordinary. I don't want to be facing the business end of a shotgun or anything because I'm taking you away from your family."

"Before Vincent, I would have said it would never happen. However, my parents are pretty mad at him for what he pulled at the wedding. So, they might be skeptical of you."

"Honestly, I would be worried if they weren't skeptical of me. If we hadn't lived through every second of this bizarre couple of weeks, I would've never believed it myself."

"What should we tell them about us?" I ask pensively, suddenly finding the messages on my cell phone unbearably interesting. This is beyond uncomfortable. *What if I have completely misread the situation and he just wants to be coworkers?*

Logan's brow furrows as he studies me. I feel like an insect at a scientific conference. "Excellent question," he comments with a shrug. "I don't know the answer. Do either of us know for sure?"

"I've been trying to figure it out myself," I hide my blush behind my hair.

Logan's eyes grow wide. "Okay, you have to tell me what thought just went through your head because the look on your face spoke volumes."

"What did it say?" I ask, curious as to what I gave away.

"I might be reading far too much into it, but what I hope it means is you've been thinking of me beyond a platonic relationship."

I decide to throw it all out there. If Logan is uncomfortable with it, I'm sure he'll let me know. "Do you want the truth?"

He nods. "That's why I asked."

"I like you a lot more than I probably should. I think about you more often than is healthy, and the things we are doing together in my dreams are definitely not platonic in nature."

"What a weird coincidence." Logan winks. "I'm having the same sort of thoughts. I was afraid it was me."

"Well, this is a happy little development," I announce with a huge grin.

"Sadly, this isn't the time or place to celebrate our breakthrough," Logan reaches for my hand and strokes the inside of my wrist.

I suck in a breath and swallow a moan as I react to the unexpected sensual touch. I drag my attention back to our conversation. "Unfortunately, this doesn't clarify the problem about what to tell my parents. My mom is a diehard matchmaker. I honestly don't know what might fly out of her mouth. Consider yourself forewarned."

Logan laughs out loud. "It could be worse; your mom could be recently divorced like my mom and hate all men with a passion."

"Sure, you say that now. Wait until my mom gives you the Inquisition about what you're going to name your babies and asks you how soon you plan to have them."

Logan grimaces. "I can see why you think it could get awkward. I'll try my best to avoid any land mines."

"Look on the bright side, you can tell my parents we are not currently dating because we haven't actually had an opportunity to go on a date yet."

"True enough. I hope to remedy that soon, though," Logan answers with a slow sexy grin.

"What does your boss think of all this?" I blurt as a

thought occurs to me. "Will he expect us to be nothing more than friends?"

"No, I don't think so. Aidan pretty much guessed there was something between us from the first moment I called him about you. I don't know how he knew unless he got a head's up from Tara."

"What would his wife know about us? As far as I am aware, I've never met her."

"I suppose this is as good a time as any to explain to you there is something extra special about Tara and Mindy. They both seem to have a gift of seeing the future. It can be disconcerting at first."

"For real? Man, I could've used some precognition skills before I got shot, it would have saved me a lot of pain and misery."

"Don't plan to use their gifts to buy lottery tickets or bet on football games, they don't utilize their gifts like that. They are pretty circumspect about what they share."

"I can imagine. It must be an awesome responsibility to know what will happen in the world but to also understand if you tell someone, you could change the course of history."

"Wow! You do get it. Tara and Mindy will be so relieved. It is often difficult for them to explain the rules of how they share what they know. They have both pretty much adopted a policy of not saying anything unless it's a matter of life and death."

"How awful for them! I'm not sure I would want to be in the position to make those kinds of calls."

"It's a difficult position to be in. I have been with each of them during times of crisis, and they both struggle with balancing everyone's needs."

"I can respect that, but wouldn't it be nice to know how we end up?" I say wistfully.

"Sometimes, but other times I think the element of surprise is powerful and can bring a couple closer together."

"You're right, I guess." We pull into my parents' driveway. "Are you ready to go face the firing squad?" I jest. However, Logan doesn't seem to get the joke as he blanches to a dusky shade of green.

"I'm kidding. I'm kidding!" I insist with a smile. "My parents are exceptionally welcoming people. If I know anything about them, I know they'll give you the benefit of the doubt."

"What if they are dead set against you moving to Oregon?"

"Then I will pull out the big guns. I'll remind them if things had gone as planned, they wouldn't have had any say over my life because I would've been married to Vinnie. That should scare the socks off them."

"Wow, you don't pull any punches, do you?"

"No, the only way they'll know I'm serious about going is if I'm honest with them about the reasons I have to leave and what I'm going into. If I can't be authentic, my parents will never believe this is for the best."

"Okay, I will follow your lead. Here's to winging it."

"Your new fella seems like a very nice young man," my mom says as we dry the dishes.

"Mom, he's not my fella yet. We are not dating."

"Nonsense!" she says sternly. "The way he looks

after you like such a gentleman tells me his feelings for you go much deeper than friendship."

"Mom, we haven't even gone there yet. Like we explained at dinner, I'm moving to Oregon for my own safety," I insist. "I am taking a job with Aidan O'Brien to help guard his niece and his protégé. It will be so much better than sitting behind a desk doing data input."

"Well, you can't blame me for worrying about your safety. The music business is dangerous — think about all the rap stars who have been killed. It seems like there's one every month in the news."

"Mom, Aidan performs classical music with some pop and country. I doubt his concerts are a hot bed of violence."

"I don't know. It makes me nervous. You know, there was that beautiful young musician killed in Florida. All she was doing was meeting fans."

"Logan is really good at his job. He has an exceptional team behind him. Aidan takes no shortcuts. He often has his wife with him on the tour. He is extremely safety conscious. Truth be told, it's probably a safer place to work than working at my local police station. At least there, I know I won't be put down because I am a woman."

"I'm not questioning your judgment, but how can you tell this for sure?" Mom presses.

"Mom, after the fiasco with Vincent, you *should* question my judgment. Everyone on the planet should question my judgment. Yet, I was really careful with this one. I talked to people who work for Silent Beats, and I had John use Identity Bank's resources to do a thorough background check on everyone involved with the company. By every measurable outcome, Aidan O'Brien and his wife run a business that should be replicated across the nation. John and I didn't run across a single employee who didn't have great things to say about Aidan O'Brien. I even talked to some local musicians from here in Florida. He was exceptionally generous with their contracts and has been flexible about working around family obligations and emergencies."

"What if you get out there and there is no real job? Then what?"

"I had a friend of John's look over the contract Aidan sent me. It is far more than fair, given my level of experience. To top it all off, Aidan gave me an advance to cover the cost of my move."

"Do you ever worry whether it's all too good to be true?" my mom asks.

"Every day. Which is why I double and triple-checked everything before I pulled up stakes to move across the country." I hesitate for a moment before I add, "It's weird I've never even been to Oregon, and in a few days, I'll live there. It's funny how life works."

My mom looks anxious for a moment. "I probably shouldn't say anything, but I have to tell you I like this young man much better than your last one. The last guy gave me the willies."

"Mom!" I exclaim. "Why didn't you say something before? I had no idea. What did Daddy think?"

"Well, your father thought he was too slick for his own good. He would grumble all the time about how Vincent is too big for his britches."

"I can't believe how much I misread this whole situation. I thought you and Daddy liked Vincent a lot. I wish you would've told me you had concerns. I could've saved bucket loads of money on the wedding that never was."

"I'm sorry, honey. I considered telling you, but then I thought better of it because who was I to rain on your parade?"

"You're my mom. I would've taken your advice," I contend.

"I know you'd like to think you would've listened because hindsight is 20/20. Knowing you, if your dad and I would've said something, you would have married Vincent even faster to prove us wrong."

I put the stack of dishes away as I stand on my tiptoes. I grimace because it's still painful to hold any amount of weight over my head. I wonder if that's ever going to go away. I turn to face my mom. "I can't argue with what you're saying. It's probably more than true. I tend to get caught up in the battle and forget I'm losing the war."

"You are tough and stubborn, for sure," my mom agrees as she pulls a bag of frozen peas out of the freezer and hands them to me to put on my shoulder. "I'm still mad at the jerk who shot you. I don't like it when you hurt," she comments when I grimace.

"I know Mom. I am mad at him too, but it doesn't do any good because he's dead." I set the bag of peas down and lead my mom over to the kitchen table and gesture for her to sit. I walk back to the counter and pour fresh cups of coffee and take them back to the table. After I sit down, I look directly at my mom. "I may not have heard you before, but I'm listening now. I need to know what you and Dad really think of Logan. I don't want you to protect me and say what you think I want to hear. I am truly at a crossroads in my life and I need to make sure I'm making the right decision."

My mom clears her throat lightly. "Now, of course my opinion of your beau is based on what your brother has told me about him and the time we spent together this evening, so take it with a grain of salt."

"I understand you haven't known him long. But, what are your initial impressions?"

"Like I said before, I think he is a very nice young man. I think he cares about you a great deal. I like the fact he is respectful of us. He does not try to interrupt you or work to prove he is right and you are wrong. He seems genuinely interested in your dad's new boat and fishing gear. That fact alone, earns him huge bonus points with your father."

"I could tell. Dad made him promise to bring me back so they could go deep sea fishing together. I guess Logan has never been, and Dad wants to be the one to introduce him to it."

"Don't be fooled, sweetie. Your dad wants to make sure you don't disappear in Oregon forever without visiting us."

"You could come out to Oregon and visit me there too. Everything I have heard and read about the place makes it sound idyllic. When it's too hot in Florida to breathe, you can come to Oregon and breathe some fresh mountain air."

"Don't you worry, your father and I plan to be frequent visitors to the West Coast."

"Mom, I know this is hard, but I appreciate your support. I will do my best to stay safe and come home to visit once my stalker has been arrested."

My mom sighs and frowns fiercely. "I've put the stalking-nastiness toward the back of my mind because I don't want to spend too much time thinking about it. It makes me so mad. I can't believe someone destroyed your car and your house."

"I know, Mom. That's why I have to leave. Aside from my family, there isn't much holding me in Florida. I just have nightmares and bad memories here now."

"I'm sorry you feel that way, Katelyn. Though I can't say I haven't felt the same. Your dad and I want you to know you have our blessing to go. Now that we have met and interacted with Logan, you have our blessing there too, if anything develops between the two of you."

"Thank you, Mom. This means the world to me. I will keep in touch. I promise."

"You better. Otherwise I'll worry myself to death."

"There is no need to be worried. Logan and I have this handled."

"Don't forget your brother. John knows things most people don't. So, if you run into trouble, you know where to find him."

"I know John has my back. He told me himself when he took me to lunch yesterday."

"I'm sorry, Katie. We don't mean to be such worrywarts, but this is such a big move. I always thought my kids would be together with me even after they grew up. I feel like a mama bird pushing the baby bird out of the nest. I hope you're ready for this."

"Mom, you know me better than that. You are not shoving me out of the nest. I am jumping out. I need to do this. I can't let someone hurt me or someone I love. Therefore, I'm removing his target. Hopefully then, he will settle down and things will go back to normal."

"I hope so too. Between you and your brother, I don't know what normal is. It's enough to make a mom's heart stop."

"I understand. I really do. But, I'll be a phone call or a text message away," I answer tearfully. "I love you guys so much. This will be one of the hardest moves I've ever made."

"I know, Katie. But, at least you have a wonderful person along for the ride. Having Logan on your side will make all the difference in the world."

I take a moment to let my mom's words sink in before I say, "I've never really thought about this before, but you're right. I am looking forward to sharing pieces of myself with Logan I never let Vinnie or anyone else see. Logan and I already have that kind of relationship. I can't imagine being with anybody else."

"In my book, 'that kind of thing' is called love," my mom announces with a soft smile.

Her simple declaration takes my breath away. It's scary to admit how true it is.

CHAPTER TWELVE

LOGAN

"I GOTTA HAND IT to you, your pick-up skills far exceed mine," Nick slaps me on the back of the shoulder. "I was hoping for a date or two while we were in town. I have to up my game plan to compete with you."

"I thought you were working things out with your hometown girl. Wouldn't that mean you need no game?"

"Negative. We're kind of in a holding pattern right now. Cheryl is trying to decide what it means for us to be a couple. I don't know why the definition is so hard. A couple means two — as in together."

"I'm sorry. Maybe she'll come to her senses sooner rather than later."

"I hope so. I hate this in between — maybe yes, maybe no stuff."

"I understand. I'd feel the same. I hope you guys can figure it out."

Nick rolls his eyes at me as he says, "You're one of *those* guys aren't you?"

"What guys?" I ask.

"You know — the guys who are all syrupy and

blissfully happy. Y'all turn into some weird relationship gurus. If you're happy, you have to preach to everyone else and make them drink the happiness Kool Aid too."

"I'm afraid you don't understand what's going on between Katie and me. I am in limbo in my relationship too. There is so much turmoil in Katie's life right now she's not sure if she is ready to try again. I don't have an answer for her — because it's true — her life is complicated and crazy right now. I don't know if I want to be the person who adds more chaos to her pile." I shrug my shoulders.

"I see," Nick responds as he takes a large step backward. "So, I suppose you wouldn't have any trouble with me stepping up to do all of her protection work — and I do mean *all*."

"Over my dead body," I announce in a lethal growl.

"Uh-huh … So, tell me again how you guys are just friends and colleagues," Nick chuckles. "I suppose next you'll tell me you want to sell me oceanfront property in the middle of Arizona."

"Lay off. It's complicated," I protest as I scrub my hand down my face.

"Complicated how? You like her and she clearly likes you. You don't even have the excuse of living in separate states anymore. Do you actually think she would be moving all the way to Oregon if the two of you were casual acquaintances? I can tell you from the way she looks at you, she feels a lot of 'something.' It seems to me the 'something' is pretty good."

"Everything about us has been complicated from the day we met. The list of issues seems insurmountable. Look at the way we met, the fact she has at least one stalker and maybe more, her precarious employment situation, and her long-term recovery from her bullet wound. She is dealing with an incredible amount of stuff," I lament.

"So are you, my brother. From what I understand, it hasn't been long since you had your own brush with death. Maybe the two of you can compare bullet wounds."

"Been there, done that. Katie's are more gnarly, but mine are more extensive."

"Dude," Nick answers sounding exasperated over my attempts at humor. "What I'm trying to tell you here is life is short. Don't take anything or anyone for granted."

"I don't plan to. I've been given an amazing opportunity to finally glue together the pieces of my life that never fit well before. I won't squander it."

"I'm so glad. I've made plenty of mistakes in my life, but I would rather my friends not make the same ones."

What is it about this process that's more exciting than a kid starting school and meeting other kindergartners for the first time? I see Katie walking toward me with a huge backpack and my heart skips a beat. I don't think I've been this giddy in a long time — if ever.

Katie drops her huge, oversized backpack at my feet. When I pick it up to put it on the bus, I practically sprain my finger as I'm trying to move it because I wasn't expecting it to be so heavy. "How in the world did you even lift this? It weighs a ton."

"I think I'm operating on adrenaline today. This is

like the fresh start I've totally needed since the shooting. I have a chance to start over where no one knows who I am or what I'm about. I don't have to live up to anyone else's expectations of me."

"I always feel optimistic at the start of a new bus tour too. It feels like the first day of school and the first day of summer camp all wrapped up into one." I rearrange some gear in the bottom of the bus to make room for her backpack.

"Is this everything you're taking with you to Oregon?" I ask with raised eyebrows.

"No, not even close. This is just what I'm taking with me for the trip. The rest of my stuff is in a shipping container on its way to Oregon."

"You were able to get your whole house packed up over the past two days? I'm sorry Nick and I couldn't help. We had back-to-back concerts and a bunch of press availability."

"It's okay. My brother had me covered," Katie explains, "Let's just say John and Tristan as a team are like logistic gurus. They had a bunch of guys packing up my house like they were professionals, making this the easiest, most straightforward move I've had since I left high school to go to college."

"For the record, I think what you've been able to pull off in a few days is miraculous," I comment as I close the hatch to the bus.

"When I asked Tristan about it, he said he was having a great time because it was like a three-dimensional game of *Tetris* to fit it all into the shipping container."

I chuckle. "If the guy loves packing that much, you can't really argue with them. You have to stand back and watch in awe."

"That's exactly what I did. I made the guys iced tea and lemonade. I got them sandwiches and chips for lunch and then I sat back and watched them dismantle my life and pack it into a big metal cube. It was extraordinary."

"I hesitate to ask this, but aside from your family, will you miss anything about Florida?"

"I'll miss Cody, for sure. He has been a great friend. On a more superficial level, I'll miss being able to go to Disney World for special occasions. It's like a ritual for me and my family. It'll be too far away now."

"I'm sorry. I promise we will come back and visit often. I don't want you to feel homesick."

"Oh, I know. I trust you. We have to find the deranged person who is terrorizing my life first though Don't get me wrong, I'm over the moon excited about moving to Oregon. The timing is perfect. I needed this change. It's a good move for me."

"Are you trying to convince me or yourself?" The side of my mouth quirks upward in a small grin.

"I don't know. Truth be told, it's probably a bit of both. It's like the gargantuan push I needed from the universe to put myself first."

"Quite a push. Someone set fire to your car and completely demolished your house — not to mention they almost killed your cat. I think there's too much to be chalked up to a push from the universe."

"I didn't exactly mean it like that. I have been doing a lot of things which are detrimental. There are certain things about life as a rookie cop, which were very hard. I couldn't put enough distance between me and the people I was trying to help, so I left pieces of my soul all over the city every day. I was feeling as if I had nothing left to give."

"I can relate. I felt much the same when I was treating soldiers in the field."

"I didn't even recognize how depleted I was until my life blew apart. I don't have much of a support system outside of my parents and John. Even though he tries to be there, my brother has been incredibly busy with his girlfriend and his new job. I didn't want to burden my family because they have been through so much. Yet, it seems every day a tiny piece of myself falls away and sometimes I begin to wonder if there's any of me left."

"Was your partner able to help you adjust to life as a rookie?"

"Cody was great. He is a phenomenal law enforcement officer. But, I didn't feel comfortable sharing details about my emotions with him because he is such a 'by the book' kind of guy. There seems to be a natural distance between us regarding professional and private matters. I never knew where to draw the line when it came to my emotions about my job. I wasn't sure if those fell on the professional side of things are on the personal side because I wasn't dealing particularly well."

"What things?" I probe, trying to understand her point of view.

"It wasn't the cases I worked which bothered me, so much as the people I couldn't help. I can't tell you the number of times I had to tell people they could file a report, but I wasn't sure if our department could do much with it. This one case still sticks out in my mind even though it happened at the very beginning of my career. A guy reported someone had broken into his shed in the back and stolen a lawnmower and weed-whacker. The monetary value of the equipment was negligible at best — because it was very, very used. Even so, to Mr. Randall, they were everything. At first, I didn't understand why someone would be so upset about a couple of missing yard implements. I later learned Mr. Randall had started his own small landscaping business after his wife died to help pay for his medical bills."

"Maybe it's me, but my first instinct would be to head down to the local hardware store and brush off my credit cards."

"That's exactly what I wanted to do! Cody told me I shouldn't become emotionally invested in my cases. He said I needed to keep a distance and perspective because I would wear myself out if I worried about every detail about all my victims."

"Much as I hate to say it, I think Cody had a point. We can't save everybody. It was the hardest thing I learned as a combat medic. I wanted to fix everything that happened to my fellow soldiers. Sometimes, injuries are too severe or too complicated to be treated on scene. Occasionally, my colleagues died right in front of me. For the longest time, every single death depressed me and haunted me for weeks if not months at a time. I finally had a CO tell me I was an *instrument* of God, not God."

"Ooh, that's blunt," Katie says sympathetically.

"I don't think he meant it to be harsh, he was joking in an offhand manner. But his words stuck with me, nonetheless. We can only do the best we can do, the rest of it is up to God, fate, or the universe."

"I suppose you're right, but I don't have to be happy about it," she concedes with a deep frown.

"True, but you also can't let it eat away at you. Like you said, if you did you would have nothing but pieces of your soul left."

"That's why this job will be so ideal for me. I am allowed to get close to the singers and their families, right?"

"Silent Beats is one large family at heart. You can get close to the people you are protecting … as long as you don't lose perspective about what threatens them."

"True. I can envision scenarios in which it would be easy to become complacent, especially if you do the same thing every day all day and don't face any active threats. It might be tempting to think you'll never face one."

"The fact you understand this simple concept puts you miles ahead of some other so-called professionals I have worked with over the years."

"I'm excited! So, when do I get to start?" Katie asks with a look of anticipation.

"You should be able to start in our next venue. Aidan is waiting for clearance from his accountant. He needs to make sure you are on the payroll and covered by our liability insurance."

Katie sighs as she gives herself a hug. "Don't mind me, I'm just having a huge fan girl moment here. I still cannot wrap my brain around the fact I'll be helping to guard Aidan O'Brien and Tasha Keeley."

"Don't forget Mindy Whitaker," I caution. "When she tours with us, she will be your primary responsibility."

"I saw Aidan perform with Tasha in Vegas a few years ago. Sadly, I'm not familiar with Mindy."

"Don't worry. You'll adore her. Mindy is all kinds of

cool. She's a little odd, but only in the best sense of the word."

"Oh, right, you told me she has some special ESP or something."

"She does. Although I don't think that's what you'll find the most challenging about Mindy," I reply with a bemused grin.

"Uh-oh, do I want to hear this?" Katie asks with trepidation.

"It's nothing bad. Mindy is unique. She's probably the smartest individual I've ever met in my life, hands down without exception. I haven't run across anything she doesn't know how to do better than everyone around her."

"I've met people like her — they are usually stuck on themselves and completely obnoxious to deal with."

"Interestingly enough, Mindy isn't. If anything, she tries to downplay the fact she is so gifted."

"How unusual. You don't see a sense of humility much anymore."

"Unusual is an extremely accurate word to describe Mindy, there isn't much typical about her."

"Thanks for the heads up. When do I get a chance to meet Mindy?"

"It'll be several days. In about nine days, we have a concert in Boulder City, right outside of Vegas. She is planning to meet us there to do a gig."

"I can't wait. This is a fun new challenge."

"Well, if you want to be there for it, you and I had better get on the bus. Word to the wise: the speakers on the bus work better on the right side than the left. Unless you want static in your ear, you should probably choose the right side of the bus."

"Cool, thanks for the heads up. Should we sit together or are we supposed to keep things more under the radar?"

I chuckle. "I don't think we can keep our relationship secret. Aidan already knows I have a thing for you. If he can figure it out from a phone call, the rest of the crew will also solve the riddle of us without much effort."

"Maybe I should let them," Katie responds with a shrug. "There are days I struggle to figure it all out. I could use some outside help."

"Trust me. The family at Silent Beats will be all up in your business. Probably more so than you ever thought possible. They will make John look like an amateur worrywart."

"You sound like you have been through this before," Katie replies with a raised eyebrow.

"It's not what you're thinking. I haven't actually been through it personally, but I have watched several friends go through it. Some cope better than others. I've noticed the people who fight it, are the people who have things to hide. If you're honest with our group, they will support you like none other. If you cross them, things do not go well."

"It sounds like there is a story there." Katie puts her hand out for me to help pull her up the large first step of the bus.

"There is a story — it's not very complicated, but it does a good job of illustrating my point. We had a sound guy who worked with Aidan for about four years. He was solid. Then he started dating someone the rest of us didn't know. He became more and more secretive as time went on. It turned out his girlfriend was a plant by one of the major tabloids, hired to dig up dirt on all of us. It was so bad, she got the scoop on our drummer and announced Liz was getting a divorce before she'd had a chance to even tell her husband."

"Oh man, that's low. On the upside, you all have a female drummer. I've always wanted to play the drums. They've been my favorite instrument since band class in elementary school."

Thinking back on a conversation we had back at the bar, I ask, "So, why don't you play drums now?"

"My dad always said if he had to spend the day driving a noisy bus, he wanted absolute silence when he got home."

"Totally understandable."

"I see that now. I can tell you as an elementary school kid and teenager, I *totally* did not understand. I probably shouldn't tell you this, but I wasn't a very nice teenager," she admits with a look of chagrin on her face.

"I can't imagine. You are the definition of nice — nice and spunky, at least."

"Well, my spunk drove my dad nuts. I used to play the television and my stereo so loud my walls would shake. My dad most certainly didn't get his dream of a quiet household when I was younger. John and I were complete maniacs."

"I was talking to John the other day, he said you both are diehard adrenaline junkies."

"I was. Up until the point where I got shot. Since then, I've been more cautious. I'm still not back to a hundred percent yet."

"You'll get there. It takes time and patience."

"I'm not big on patience. I'm an instant gratification junkie. Hence, I find the process of physical therapy very frustrating. I want to be making miles and miles of progress; instead, everything is measured in millimeters. I don't want my progress to be measured in something so small I can barely see it. I want to be back to where I was and get even stronger. Sadly, that I haven't. It's enough to drive me batty."

"When we get home, I will hook you up with a talented physical therapist. This guy saved my sanity. When I first got shot, I could barely move. But he made all the difference in the world. Hopefully, he can help you."

Katie stares at me blankly. "I'm sorry, I stopped listening to you after I heard the phrase 'when we get' home. Hearing you say that blows my mind. Think about it — just a couple of weeks ago, I was set to marry someone else and lead a whole different lifestyle."

"Are you sorry you didn't get married?" I ask in a moment of profound self-doubt.

"No, not at all. My thoughts were quite the opposite. I suspect I dodged a bullet of a whole different kind. I can't wait to 'go home' as you put it."

"It's funny what a little perspective will do for us. I am so glad you came with me. Oregon will feel even more like home to me."

CHAPTER THIRTEEN

KATIE

"I ADMIRE YOUR COURAGE." Tasha is trying on new clothes in the wardrobe room. "I don't know if I would have been brave enough to move clear across the country."

"It was actually a pretty easy decision for me. Things are potentially deadly back in Florida. They still can't identify my stalker. Since my insurance company gets cranky about cars being turned into shish-kebabs, it makes much more sense for me to leave the area."

"Don't take this the wrong way or anything, but are you sure your stalker isn't your mother?" Tasha asks with a smirk.

"No! Are you kidding? My mom won't even jaywalk."

"Just saying, it's good to rule out crazy family members. Been there, done that and bought the T-shirt."

"That sucks. I would be happy to loan you my mom. She's like a mother to all my friends. So, one more wouldn't hurt."

"Aidan's gang has taken good care of me. They

have adopted me into the Girlfriend Posse."

"Girlfriend Posse? Sounds promising. I'm sick of operating in a male-dominated world right now."

"It is probably the coolest thing I have ever encountered. It started with Aidan's wife, Tara, and her two best friends pledging to always have each other's back. Over the years, it has grown to include several other women."

"What do you do, have tea and cookies or something?"

"Only if we meet at Gwendolyn's house, the rest of the time we typically stuff our faces with junk food. If we meet at Joy and Tiers, Heather's bakery, the eats are seriously good."

"So, you get together and eat while you gab?" I ask, confused about the purpose behind the Girlfriend Posse.

"Sometimes we do that, but most of the time, we are trying to solve someone's problem."

"What kind of problems?" I probe, suddenly very curious about a strong group of women helping each other.

"It can be huge like when everyone got together to support Gwendolyn when she had lung cancer or when someone gets married and needs us to pull off a wedding in a week, or it can be something little like when Mindy wanted us to go prom dress shopping with her."

"Sounds cool. So, what do I have to do to join this Girlfriend Posse?"

"I don't know if there are any formal membership requirements or anything. I was kinda adopted into it because of my relationship with Aidan."

"Maybe they'll adopt me too. That would be great. Other than Logan, I don't really have any friends here."

"Well, you have Mindy and me. Having you join Tara's self-defense class has encouraged me to kick it up a notch. Mindy and I will be bad-to-the-bone when you guys are through with us."

"It's been a while since I've been able to enjoy exercise and working out. Sparring with Tara has been far more fun than it should be."

"How is your recovery going?"

"Sometimes I'm sore because I developed some adhesions after surgery, but the doctors think eventually the inflammation in my shoulder will go down and I will get my dexterity back. I'm almost one hundred percent. There is a little catch in my draw and it is frustrating. I used to be one of the best shots in the whole gun range."

"Ooh, how did the guys in your unit react? Some guys get their feelings hurt when they get beat."

"Some of them, like my partner Cody, were really supportive. Others, not so much. There was this one guy who swore I must cheat on my tests. I'm not exactly sure how you cheat at a gun range when it's just you and a target — but, whatever."

Tasha rolls her eyes. "I used to run into that kind of attitude all the time when I competed in pageants. Some people are sore losers. You can't let them steal your sunshine."

"That's a good term for what was happening to me. It was like I couldn't even be proud of my own accomplishments because other people would call me a witch."

"Well, if you run into it here, let me know. Silent Beats isn't that type of organization."

"Yeah, I've noticed. I have been accepted here like I've always been part of the team. I didn't know if it's because Logan and I are dating or if it's because everyone respects my skills here."

"To be honest, it's probably a bit of both. The fact Logan loves you and thinks enough of you to bring you on the team speaks well for you. It probably gives you some credibility you might not have had on your own."

"I get that, but even though Logan and I are a couple, people treat me like I have value outside of my relationship with Logan. It's a refreshing change."

"I didn't want to ask, because I don't want to seem rude, but someone told me you were engaged before you met Logan. Does Logan think all the threats against you are because you broke up with your previous fiancé?"

"Most of the evidence points in that direction. Unfortunately, no one is really sure."

"You guys have been in Oregon for a month or so, have there been any more threats against you?"

"I don't talk to Vincent at all anymore. I blocked his whole family on social media after the wedding fiasco."

"Oh, I totally understand. When we were trying to figure out who my stalker was, I didn't know who I could trust. I found it hard to figure out who were my real friends, and which were my enemies. It was scary."

"How did you keep your sanity? I'm having trouble sleeping. I look over my shoulder all the time. The scary thing is I don't even know who I'm looking for. You would think as a police officer, I would have a better sense of things, but I don't."

"Maybe you're too close to the situation to see all the clues. Jude kept me sane. Actually, it was Jude and Logan working together. At one point, Logan had to take my phone away and limit my Internet access so I couldn't be attacked."

"Yeah, Logan has a fiercely protective streak, and he can get bossy if he thinks you are in danger."

"Tell me about it! The phone thing turned out to be a good thing because it limited my mother's access to me. I was much happier without her constant critical voice in my ear."

"Maybe your mom is related to my ex-fiancé, it sounds like the two of them are cut from the same cloth," I comment with a grim smile. "The last straw for me was when Vinnie decided he would be a better fashion consultant than the professionals who helped me pick my dress. I loved my dress, but he hated every inch of it. Then, to add insult to injury, he didn't want me to wear my grandmother's wedding veil. Who does that?"

"A narcissistic jerk who thinks the world revolves around him?" Tasha responds.

"That about sums him up too. I think you might be right about being too close to the situation. I mean, look at what I've been through. As a law enforcement officer, I'm well educated on how to spot a domestic violence situation, but I didn't even realize I was in an emotionally abusive relationship until it was almost too late."

"I know for me, I knew I was being abused by my

mom, but I didn't want to let the whole world know what a colossal mess my personal relationships were. So, I let a lot of things slide that I should've never put up with. It took Jude pointing out to me — sometimes every day — how abusive my mom's words were. I was used to hearing them my whole life, and I didn't know how to put them into perspective. But, Jude's comments made me focus on how terrible the things my mom said about me for years were. Finally, I decided my sanity and my relationship with Jude were so much more important than holding up appearances."

"I think you hit it spot on. I wanted the appearance of being in a happy relationship. I forgot about the fact it's a lot easier to survive in a relationship when you are actually happy instead of pretending to be happy."

"I take it those days are over now? You and Logan seem content together. In all the years I have known the man, I have never seen him smile so much. I hope you are not faking it with him."

"I'm not pretending to be happy with Logan. I'm having a great time being someone's true partner in life for a change."

"I can't tell you how happy I am to hear that. Logan is like a big brother to me. I consider him to be more of a family than my actual family. If I thought you were setting out to hurt him, you and I would have to have a 'come to Jesus' meeting and sort it all out."

"You sound like me! When my big brother started dating his fiancée, I went ballistic. I was completely skeptical of Tayanita. I was certain she'd take advantage of John."

Tasha laughs softly. "So, what's your relationship now?"

"My relationship with Tayanita is great now. She and John have been together for a couple of years now. Shortly after I met her, I realized all my concerns were pretty much invalid. She has turned out to be a great partner for John."

"What does John think of your move to Oregon?" Tasha asks.

"Let's say Logan has been vetted enough he could probably work for the Secret Service now. My brother and the company he works for are pretty thorough."

"How did Logan take all the poking around? Was he offended?"

"Nope. Logan told John when his sisters start to date someone he'll hire John to do the same kind of background check on them. He totally understood. In fact, it was a bit of a bonding experience for John and Logan."

Tasha grins. "Men are so weird."

I sigh. "True, but I'm sure glad I have this particular man in my life. He makes it possible for me not to despise a whole gender."

"There are some good guys out there, but they are hard-to-find. In my experience, once you find the right guy, all the puzzle pieces in your life fit so much better."

"Logan, what are you doing? You are never getting all those clothes in a duffel bag unless you roll them. Why are you packing clothes?" I ask as I watch Logan trying to stuff all manner of clothing into a large duffel bag.

"Well, my little adrenaline junkie, I have plans for us this weekend," Logan announces with a smug grin.

"You do? I thought you had to work this weekend."

"Initially, I was on the schedule, but Nick swapped with me so I could spend the weekend with you."

"Good of him," I comment.

"Yeah, he volunteered to do me a solid. I don't know what he'll want in the future, but I'm not going to worry about that today. Today is for enjoying ourselves immensely."

"That's all you're saying? You're not gonna give me any clue about where we're going? How do I know you are packing me the right things?"

Logan grins. "I suppose you don't. This might be the ultimate trust-building exercise between the two of us."

"Oh, you are fifty-thousand different kinds of mean," I protest. I walk up to Logan and give him a deep kiss. "Are you sure there's nothing I can do to make you change your mind?" I ask suggestively.

"Quite the interrogation technique you have there, Officer Ashford, but I'm not biting. It's a secret until we get there."

I stick my bottom lip out in a pout as I respond, "You're no fun!"

"Not true. I'm all sorts of fun. You're just mad I'm not feeding your need for instant gratification."

I stick my tongue out at him. "I think it's in my best

interest to remain silent. I might be guilty as charged. Seriously … where are we going?"

"Somewhere where you need a coat," he replies cryptically.

"*Arrgh!* This is Oregon! I need a coat everywhere. Some clues would be nice."

Logan draws me into a loose embrace. "I'm sorry to have to keep you in suspense, but trust me — it will be worth it. By the way, I wasn't just giving you a clue. You really do need a coat."

"But, I saw you pack two sweatshirts and our Under Armor. Won't that be enough?" I ask, trying to draw out more details from Logan.

He doesn't fall for my bait. "Better to be safe than sorry."

"You're impossible!" I exclaim.

"Yeah, I am. You love me anyway," Logan counters as he zips up the duffel bag and slings it over his shoulder. "Come on, let's go we're burning daylight."

I hear Logan call my name. "Katie, you might want to wake up for this." When I open my eyes, I realize we must've been driving for a long while. The sun is in a whole new position. I pull my seat back up to an upright position and peek out the window. I gasp at what I see.

"The ocean? You brought me to see *the ocean*. So cool!" As I take a closer look at the window, I realize we are driving near the edge of a cliff. There is a sheer drop off mere feet from the highway.

"Where are your beaches? There's no sand to play on," I say as I look out over the scenery.

"The sand is not the same in Oregon as it is in Florida. It feels very different. Some areas have more beach access than others."

"Oh, too bad. I like to play on the beach. It's one of my favorite things to do."

"Just because there is no beach access at this moment, doesn't mean there isn't plenty of sand where we're going."

"Are you sure? There doesn't seem to be enough beach to go around."

"I'm sure," he answers with a serene smile.

I see a sign as we drive down the highway. "You have a national forest called Swiss Law?"

"No, it says Siuslaw — like *sigh-oos-law*. It's a Native American word," Logan says as he returns off the highway and onto a winding road. After several minutes, we pull into a parking lot.

As Logan helps me out of the car, a blast of wind hits my face. "Now I get why you wanted me to bring a coat."

Logan pulls the duffel bag out of the back and pulls a heavy sweatshirt out for me. "I think you'll probably want to put this on under your jacket."

"Really? Are we going ice cave diving?"

"Nope, we'll save the spelunking for another adventure. I have something more action-packed for us. I hope you don't mind helmet hair."

"Mind it? Are you kidding? You are looking at a

diehard BMX racer. John and I used to race when we were younger. I don't mind saying, I beat the pants off my brother. So, you are now forewarned, I am a whiz with anything involving wheels."

"Oh good. So, you'll probably love driving a sand buggy."

I stop in my tracks. "I suppose it depends. Are you actually letting me drive my own buggy or do I have to sit and watch you show off for me?"

Logan looks genuinely puzzled. "Of course you're driving your own buggy. Why wouldn't you?"

"I'm sorry, I'm thinking back on this awful date I had with Vincent once. He took me to one of those 'drive like a NASCAR driver' camps, but he didn't want me to participate, he wanted to show me how great he was."

"I'm surprised you stood for that kind of thing. You could probably drive circles around him because of your training in the police academy."

"I tried to explain that to him, but he wasn't listening. He created a scene. Since I was stranded thousands of miles from home, I couldn't say anything. The airline tickets were in his name. If I would've stood up for myself, he could've very easily destroyed those and left me stranded."

"Wow! Everything I learn about Dear-ol'-Vinnie makes him seem like more and more of a complete and total jerk, if not a monster."

"You know, in retrospect I see everything so clearly. But when I was living it, it just seemed like he was upset because of something I did and I needed to watch my actions more closely. It's textbook verbal abuse. Yet, when I was experiencing it, I blamed myself, like virtually every other abuse victim. You would think I would know better." I slump against him in defeat.

"Katie, one of the things I learned serving in the military is sometimes your assessment of the situation when you're right in the middle of it is completely different when you can pull back and see it from a distance. You forget Vinnie was playing with your mind. He knew exactly how to break you down and make you feel weak. By the time you figured out he was playing those kinds of mind games, you were already knocked back on your heels."

"That's just it Logan, I should have known and I didn't see it. Maybe I didn't see the warning signs in the lives of crime victims either. I wonder if my inability to see what was really going on is only the tip of the iceberg. What if I don't have the skills to be a law enforcement officer?"

"Katie, your instincts are sharp. Cody had nothing but nice things to say about you and your police work. You got a commendation from your city because you kept your wits about you. All evidence confirms you were a spectacular cop."

"For a rookie, you mean?" I tease.

"Everybody learns something from every case they handle, but Cody could do nothing but sing your praises. He doesn't strike me as the kind of officer who would embellish someone's story just for points."

"No, Cody is not an officer who seeks out drama and conflict. He's a by-the-book straight as an arrow kind of cop. I am honored he thought I was following in his footsteps. I feel so stupid for falling for the likes of Vincent."

"I don't think you need to, but you can't change the way you feel," Logan says as he pulls my hood up over my head and pulls the drawstrings tight.

I give myself a mental shake. "Enough of this serious talk, I'm ready to fly off some hills and leave you in my dust," I promise as I give him a cheesy grin.

"My only thought is the same one I've had since the day I met you."

"I don't know if I want to hear this," I remark with trepidation in my voice.

"It's nothing bad, I promise. I knew if I got involved with you, I'd probably spend a lot of time chasing you — the only question was for how long …"

CHAPTER FOURTEEN

LOGAN

"I CAN'T BELIEVE THE maneuvers you were doing on Showoff Hill. Talk about giving me an anxiety attack," I comment as I try to brush the sand off Katie.

"What are you talking about? I only bit the dust once, and it was because I wasn't familiar with the throttle. It stuck a little. Once I figured that out, I was golden."

"I know you were. You were like poetry in motion. I've never seen somebody move a sand buggy with as much ease as Tara has when she dances."

Katie motions for me to turn around so she can brush my backside off. "My, oh my, there is a lot of sand there. One would think you might've crashed and burned a few dozen times," she teases.

"Hey, my mom didn't raise no dummy. I know when to graciously concede defeat. You were beyond phenomenal. I'm so proud of you. It was so fun to see you go all out full-throttle with a smile from ear to ear."

"I told you — I was born to drive things with wheels."

"Something tells me if I took you skiing, you would probably beat the pants off me on the mountain too. I think you are a force of nature."

"Well, I've been called worse things. I'll take it." Katie grins.

I clasp her hand and interlace my fingers through hers as we walk back over to the car. "Thank you for this. It's been a long time since I have been able to hang out with someone and be myself. I love spending time with you."

"This is the most fun I've had in years. I'm glad I could share it with you. We can come back here any time," she remarks.

"How about we grab some lunch? I didn't plan to spend quite this much time out here. Quite frankly I thought we would be chased away by the weather. I need to check my blood sugar in a cleaner place. I feel like I've got sand in every crevice."

"I know this is rude and probably presumptuous of me to ask, but do we have a room here? If we do, I could use a shower before dinner. It sounds like you may need one worse than I do."

"As a matter of fact, I got us a room. We have reservations at the River House. It's right downtown. So, we can visit the shops tomorrow."

"What are we doing tonight?" Katie asks with a frown.

"Does the thought of a hot tub in our room make you happy?" I reply.

"Like you wouldn't believe!" Katie exclaims. "I might be made to drive anything with wheels, but it's been a while since I've done anything but defensive driving school. These muscles will scream in pain in a few hours."

"My thoughts were following a slightly different path, but whatever works," I answer with a wink.

"Where did you find this place? The food is out of this world," Katie gushes as she steals a bite of my salmon.

I shrug. "I always do online research before I go someplace to make sure they have stuff I can eat. The menu here sounded especially enticing."

"It's a shame you can't have the chowder. It is scrumptious."

"I can have a bite or two, but there are too many carbs for me to have a whole bowl."

"Before I met you, I thought I was a healthy eater. You put me to shame. I guess that's one great perk about dating you. Even though we eat out a lot, I am still losing weight because I'm following your example."

I grimace. "Don't make me out to be too much of a hero. I eat this way because it makes me feel better. Before the bullets took out most of my pancreas, I had abysmal eating habits. It was a hard adjustment for me. I have a passionate crush on pizza crust and bagels. The change was hard."

"There are so many things I would miss if it were me. I haven't met a potato I don't like — fries, baked, mashed, steamed or loaded — I like them all. I think I would feel deprived after a while," she replies wistfully.

"Sometimes I do, but usually it's only at family gatherings where there are a bunch of people there with different food tastes. Birthday parties are hard for me because I like cake and it's one of those things that's difficult to make sugar-free and still taste good. Occasionally, I feel like I'm outside a pet store window looking in at the puppy I've always wanted."

"I'm sad for you. Can you get one of those machines that automatically gives you insulin?"

"I'm waiting for my insurance to sort it all out. The Army isn't real keen on providing insulin pumps to people because they are expensive. My private insurance doesn't want to pick up the cost of the surgery because they say my military insurance should be able to cover it through the VA."

"I saw a television show where a guy was competing on an obstacle course with one of those and he said it changed his life."

"I have friends who have pumps and they say it's made a world of difference for them. I have to say, I'm very tempted to pay the cost out of my pocket."

"Hard decision. It's weird, I don't think about your diabetes much. You seem to manage it pretty discreetly."

"I'm sure there is a compliment in there somewhere," I respond with a quirk of my lips.

"Make no mistake, it was a total compliment. I had a great aunt who had diabetes. She made a huge production of testing her blood sugar and announcing all the ways she suffered and every insulin shot she ever took."

I shrug. "That's never been my style. I like to fly under the radar."

"Do most people even know you have diabetes?"

"I don't tell everyone, but I do wear a medic alert bracelet. Most people don't notice it."

"I feel foolish because when we first met, I didn't notice either. To make matters worse, I made all sorts of unfair assumptions about why you left the military. You would think having a brother with a disability and being a police officer would make me more sensitive. But, I did it anyway. I'm embarrassed by my idiotic behavior."

I reach out and squeeze Katie's hands. "Don't be. Before I became part of the club of people with invisible disabilities, I didn't really know the difference. Of course, I'd heard the term, but I didn't know what it meant in everyday life."

"You're lucky, it doesn't seem to impact your life as much as it did my great aunt. She had a list a mile and a half long of all the foods she wasn't allowed to eat because they would bother her sugars. Usually, she would go ahead and eat the foods on the list anyway because she wasn't letting any doctors tell her what she could and could not eat. It was frustrating to see her do things which harmed her."

"I will admit, sometimes it's hard to make the right choices. My list is probably equally long; I just work around it. Aidan is good at making sure there's a wide variety of food around."

"Good. At the police station, we didn't always eat so well. It was like junk food central. I'm glad Silent Beats is so supportive."

"Yeah, it's great; but I have worked for other employers who have not been so accommodating. Right after I went back to work after my incident, I was working security for a pretty high-end department store. They fired me after they found out about my diagnosis," I admit as I take a sip of my black coffee.

"Why?" Katie asks with a befuddled look.

"Great question. The reason the company gave was some mumbo-jumbo about me messing up their shared risk pool for insurance. What a ridiculous, bogus reason since I don't typically go to the doctor more often than anyone else."

"Wow! You could probably sue or something. I'm sure that sort of crap is illegal."

"It is, but I wasn't willing to admit my weaknesses yet. I was still in the mindset diabetes was a chink in my armor. I was afraid having diabetes would somehow make me fragile. I didn't know how I would cope with what I thought was an old person's disease."

"Must've been really frustrating. I can't imagine what it would be like to lose control over something as basic as your blood sugar. I know before I was shot, I took the simple act of breathing for granted. After I broke several ribs and punctured a hole in a blood vessel leading to my heart, I value each breath I take a little more."

"I value the breaths you take too. Would you like some dessert?"

Katie looks longingly at the dessert list. "Go ahead. I'm used to seeing people eat in front of me, it's no big deal," I tease as I push the menu in front of her. "If their desserts are anything like their dinners, it would be a shame to pass them up."

"No, it's okay. I am beyond stuffed from dinner. I

would rather take a walk on the beach."

"Should be better now," I say as I zip up my oversized fleece jacket over the top of Katie's sweatshirt and coat.

"Thank goodness it's still warm from your body heat. I can't believe how cold it is out here. It's like Florida in the dead of winter. How do you all cope?"

Katie's teeth are chattering violently, and I tuck her in beside me as we walk down the tide line. "I guess you get used to the rain and cold in the Pacific Northwest. This is typical for us. Aidan's friend, William, has a cottage on the beach. He says the secret to surviving the Oregon coast is to wear lots and lots of layers."

"I don't think there are enough layers on the planet to keep me warm. The wind goes right through me."

"We can go in if you'd like?" I suggest.

"No, I want to be here. I'm just surprised it's so cold on a beautiful day."

"Okay, I was just checking. If you get too cold, let me know."

A group of horseback riders passes us, and Katie's eyes light up. "Someday, I want to do that! I've seen it in the movies, and it looks like the coolest thing ever but, I've never done it."

"Aidan's friends, Heather and Tyler have horses, but I've never ridden them on the beach. I've only ridden them when I helped Aidan out with his day camp for the junior high school kids. The thing I learned from that lesson is teenage girls can scream very loud in your ear. I thought maybe it was a concert thing, but I've since learned otherwise."

"Find someone who was afraid of horses, did you?"

"Yes, she was terrified. She didn't want to lose face in front of her friends, so she toughed it out, and by the end of the day, she was having fun. Still, the beginning was not fun at all."

"I can imagine! I don't think I would be afraid to ride a horse on the beach. After all, I do almost everything else. I like to race go carts and I'm into BMX bikes. It doesn't seem like horses would be any scarier."

"Okay, I'll see what I can do to help make your dream come true," I reply. "It might take another visit to the coast, but I think we can get it done."

"If it means we get to eat at Bridgewater Fish Market again, sign me up anytime," she says as she rubs her stomach. "They have some of the best food I've had anywhere."

"I agree. I didn't realize until tonight that you are such a foodie."

Katie tucks her hair behind her ear as she says, "I don't have much time to cook but, I like to watch all the television shows about cooking. I learned a bunch. When I was growing up, I was a big fan of Julia Child's shows on PBS."

"Maybe this job will be less time-consuming than being a rookie at the PD. I know if it's anything like the military, if you're the newcomer, everybody craps all over you and makes you take all the terrible shifts."

"It's true. I had to work every single holiday ever invented," Katie agrees. "I won't miss that part of the job, for sure." Katie scans the beach for shells and pretty rocks to give to her soon-to-be-niece, Ketki. Suddenly, Katie takes off down the beach as she announces, "Look! There is a campfire site here. Is it all right if we light a fire?"

"As long as it doesn't use driftwood, it's legal to have a fire. Those look like leftover Presto logs. So, I think we'd be legal. Unfortunately, I don't have any matches with me. It is too cold for me to light one by hand although I do have the skills to do it, if push comes to shove."

Katie shrugs off her backpack. "I know you think it's funny I carry this everywhere, but I'm actually prepared for anything," she proclaims as she triumphantly hands me a Zippo lighter.

"Okay, I'm totally impressed because you don't even smoke. Do you carry it around with you just in case we stumble across a campfire?" I laugh.

Katie sticks her tongue out at me. "Well, it works, doesn't it? I have a veritable survival pack here."

"I don't suppose you have any marshmallows in there so we can make some s'mores," I hint with a grin.

She shakes her head. "Sadly I don't. The only ingredients used to make s'mores I have are a few stray Hershey's bars left over from Halloween."

I wrinkle my nose. "Yum ... tasty."

"What's that face for? They're wrapped and kept in a plastic bag."

"Okay, good. Mindy's little brother, Charlie, dug one out of his mom's purse, and it was a little worse for the wear. Charlie didn't care, he ate it anyway."

Katie shrugs. "Most kids don't. I try to keep myself organized and tidy. Otherwise, my backpack becomes the great abyss."

I stumble as I'm suddenly hit by double vision. As I try to right myself, I notice I am feeling shaky all over.

Katie is arranging the logs on the campfire. I place my hand on her shoulder as I say, "I'm sorry, I can't do this right now. We have to go back to the room."

"Why?" she says with a puzzled look on her face. "Are you cold since I took your jacket?"

"No, I left my glucose meter and tabs back in the room, and my blood sugars are bottoming out," I explain in a somewhat weak voice.

"That's not good, right?" Her eyes widen. "Is there anything I can do?" she digs through her backpack and comes up with a pack of gum and the Hershey's bars. "This is all I've got, but will it help?"

"It'll do until we get back to the hotel room," I say as I reach out to grab the candy. "I'm a little mortified."

"Don't be, this isn't your fault. It's not like you got yourself drunk on Jack Daniels or anything," she teases.

"Good point," I concede as I break the candy bar into pieces and eat them. "I'm sorry to cut our date short, but I need to go back to the room."

"Hey, don't worry about it. I'm getting cold, anyway. Besides, didn't we have plans to soak in the hot tub tonight? I mean, we've got one right in our room. How cool is that?" Katie grabs my hand and helps me up. This time, as we walk up the shoreline, she is supporting me.

"Didn't you take your blood sugar a few minutes ago?" Katie asks as she flips through the channels on the TV. "Doesn't it hurt to test so often?"

"I don't know exactly what happened today. Maybe I got too dehydrated, or perhaps I was drinking too much coffee. It could have been because we spent so much time running up and down the sand dunes. But, for whatever reason, my blood sugar crashed big-time. Now, I am testing my blood to make sure it's in the right zone. Sometimes, if I compensate by eating too much sugar, I can create a situation where I need to take more insulin."

"Sounds complicated. Don't you get frustrated?"

"Sometimes, especially after I just bragged to you about how carefully I control my blood sugar levels. Nothing like nature making me look like a fool."

"Yeah, must be frustrating. I watched what you ate today, and it looked clean to me. You were eating so healthy, it made me feel like a junk food addict. You didn't even have any breading on your fish."

I shrug. "Every once in a while, a crash will happen and I won't know why. Diabetes is so complicated. It's not about having the same numbers every single day even if you have pretty standard routines. Everything can affect it. Sometimes, the first indication I'll have if I'm getting sick is my numbers will be all over the place. I can tell something nasty is afoot."

"So basically what you're telling me is we could have ordered a yummy dessert tonight, huh?"

"In retrospect, probably, but I didn't know it at the time."

"It would be nice to be able to see into the future, wouldn't it?" Katie asks as she tenderly strokes the side of my face.

Instinctively, I lean toward her touch. "For more reasons than you could possibly know."

Chapter Fifteen

Katie

I RINSE OFF A washcloth and squeeze it out. I guess it's a common side effect, but I wasn't prepared for Logan to be drenched in sweat. I'm trying to make him as comfortable as possible. At the moment, he has a massive headache. He says it's because his blood sugar bottomed out. Though he showed me that his meter indicated his blood sugar had returned to the normal zone, I am still nervous. I wonder if he needs to go to the hospital or anything.

I know if I had a moment to call John, he would tell me not to mother my boyfriend to death. If Logan says he's fine, he probably is. Still, it was frightening to see Logan struggle to find words and be confused about where our room was.

Aside from a headache and the sweating, he seems better. He can follow our conversation now and was even arguing with the commentator on television. I thought I was the only person who had conversations with my technology. I often argue with my own television or computer. It's reassuring to know I am in good company.

I wrap up the other half of the sandwich he ate and

put it in the refrigerator. I was afraid getting food would be hard, but once I explained to the hotel manager why we needed a sandwich after room service had closed, the kitchen staff were very responsive and made him a sandwich with lots of meat right on the spot.

I pull out one of my historical romance novels we picked up on our walk through downtown before dinner. I don't even know how Logan knew about my weakness for romance novels. But, he chose three new ones I didn't have and checked out while I was looking for other things to send to my family. It was a wonderful surprise to find the books laying on the bed when we came back from our walk.

I'm still not used to the climate in Oregon, so I put on a T-shirt under my flannel pajamas and curl up next to Logan on the bed. He is sleeping much better now than he was a few minutes ago. His sweating has stopped, and his breathing has evened out.

I read until my eyes get heavy. As I lean over to put my book on the nightstand, Logan's eyes open abruptly. "I'm sorry. I wanted to be like one of your romantic, conquering heroes. Instead, I crashed and burned. I know you have no reason to believe me, but this does not happen very often. Usually, my blood sugar is much more stable."

"Even if it weren't stable, it wouldn't matter to me. As long as I know what's coming, I can pretty much cope with anything. I will admit it was scary, but now that I've seen it happen, I'll be better prepared for the next time."

Logan closes his eyes and flops his arm over his face as he says, "This is still not how I planned to spend our evening together. I had a much more sensual itinerary in mind."

"We'll have plenty of time for that in the future. This is only one day, we'll have lots and lots of days together, and we can try again some other time when you are feeling like your usual self."

"Maybe you're right. I hope this is a temporary glitch and we will laugh about it someday, but today it sucks."

I hop off the bed and walk over to the ice bucket. "It's a little melted now, but I got you some ice earlier. There are some plastic bags here, would an ice pack for your head, be helpful?"

Logan nods as he says, "Yes, that would be great. This headache is a pain."

"I know. If I could wave a magic wand, I would make it all go away."

I pour some ice in a plastic bag and triple knot the top. I wrap it in a towel and carefully place it on his forehead.

"I have to tell you Vinnie-the-Pooh was not only a jerk, he was a fool. You are a phenomenal girlfriend. This is probably wrong of me to say, but I'm glad he was too stupid to see that."

"Me too," I concede. "Life with you is much better, even though there might be a bump or two in the road."

I must've been exhausted. I didn't even hear Logan's watch alarm go off. *Crap!* I didn't even think about setting it for him. Maybe he slept through his testing. Some girlfriend I am. I should have been paying more attention. There is a reason my soon-to-be sister-in-law is a nurse and I am not.

I reach over to check Logan and find the bed empty. Panicked, I bolt straight out of bed. I nearly have a heart attack when I hear Logan say in a low rumbling voice, "Can I help you with something?"

Scrambling to put my glasses on, I glance around the room and find him calmly typing away on his computer.

I collapse down on the bed. "Don't mind me. I was having a massive anxiety attack when I couldn't find you in bed next to me. I was really worried about you. Last night was dicey there for a while."

"I'm sorry. I didn't mean to worry you. My body doesn't cooperate well with the concept of being on vacation. Even if I try to sleep in, I struggle. I guess it's too many years on the road. The weekends are typically my busy time."

"I wondered how we were both able to take this weekend off."

"Aidan and Tara are dealing with some personal stuff, so Aidan has cut back his touring quite a bit."

"I like Tara and Aidan a lot. Is there anything I can help with?"

"Unfortunately, I think it's something they have to solve themselves. It's hard for the rest of the team because we can't help and we all would like to. It's difficult to sit on the sidelines and watch it all unfold."

"I'm sorry. You were right, this team feels very much like a family. Let me know if I can help. I know I'm the newcomer, but sometimes fresh eyes on a problem can make the difference."

"It might if this was related to security, but it's more of a personal thing between the two of them. They have to sort it out. It's taken a toll on them. That's why I have been supportive of Aidan cutting back on his schedule."

"It must be nice for you too. I have a feeling you don't take much time off."

"I can't argue with you. It's an accurate assessment of me. You're right, there is a silver lining to all the stuff that's going on. I plan to take full advantage of it today."

"Tell me more," I prompt

"Well, you might not know this about me, but I like to grant wishes. How about we check off something on your bucket list?"

"You know, that phrase has a whole new meaning for me now that I have been shot. I used to think of my bucket list as something I would complete when I was much older. However, recent experiences have taught me you can be close to death at any age. So, I'm looking at my vast list of things to do before I die a little more carefully."

"Well, I hope the item I've chosen to do today is still on your list because it seems phenomenally fun."

"Are we going hot air ballooning?" I guess.

"Nope, not today; it's too windy. I didn't even know that was on your to-do list."

"Windy? Is there a kite festival somewhere close? Flying one of those big box kites is on my bucket list too."

"That's not on tap for today either. However, we can put it on our itinerary of things to do. I think Aidan has some gigs booked at the casino, so I can look around and see when the local festivals are. Maybe the dates coincide."

"Epic."

"Is there anything else you'd like to do?"

"I don't know if I'm quite up to this yet in my recovery because I'm having a hard time with the range of motion in my shoulder. Our conversation last night reminded me how much, I'd like to go skiing. I heard you guys have fantastic skiing here."

"I haven't been in a while. I'm not an expert or anything, I do it for fun. You'll probably have to confine me to the bunny slopes."

"It's been so long for me, I'll probably have to hit the beginner slopes too."

"The next time we have a long weekend in Portland, I'll see if we have a big enough group to rent a house near Timberline Lodge."

"It's been forever since I've been on a group date — it sounds fun. Enough suspense! If you're not taking me spelunking, kite flying or skiing, what are we doing today?" I feel like the kid who kicks the back of the seat all the way to the destination incessantly repeating 'Are we there yet?'.

Logan walks over to me and starts rubbing my shoulders as he leans down and murmurs in my ear, "I think it would be more fun to surprise you than to tell you. So, all I'll say is, 'Dress warmly in several layers.'"

"Well, I guess it's a good thing we stopped by the outlet store. I got myself some running gear because I have ambitious intentions. In order to chase after any potential bad guys, I need to be in shape. Working a desk job has been disastrous for my fitness level."

"I understand. My rehab from my gunshot wound was long and arduous. I lost a lot of muscle mass. If you need a running partner, I'll be happy to join you."

"It's a pity for you I'm going to have a lot more clothes on when I run on this coast than when I ran in Florida," I tease with what I hope is a come-hither look.

"That's okay, I've got a phenomenal imagination. Besides, the running gear you got can be pretty form-fitting. I might not have to imagine much."

"Oh, great! Way to make a girl who needs to lose a few pounds feel good about herself. Now running in front of you will make me feel self-conscious," I protest as I dart out of his arms and start to sort through my bags for clothes to wear.

He places his hand on my shoulder and turns me toward him as he looks in my eyes. "That is one thing you can cross off your list of worries. I'll think you are smoking hot regardless of what you weigh. Attitude means more to me than body weight."

"Lucky for you I've got attitude in spades," I retort as I make a funny face. "I still can't believe you're not telling me where we're going? That's just so mean!"

"I'm not worried. I suspect you will completely forgive me once we get there — but we better hurry because they're expecting us in about an hour."

"How fortunate I don't spend a lot of time on hair and makeup," I smirk.

"What I said before about your weight, also applies to your makeup. Do whatever makes you happy. For today I might recommend a ponytail. The wind is pretty wicked out there."

"Okay, I'm off to take a shower, but we need to figure out what we're doing about breakfast. Yesterday taught me all I ever need to know about you drinking too much coffee and skipping meals."

"Don't worry about it, I've got it covered. Room service should be up shortly with our breakfasts."

"Oh, I hope you ordered the strawberry crepes for me. They look amazing on the menu."

"Of course I did; I paid attention when you were drooling all over the menu yesterday."

I walk over and give Logan a hug from behind as I confess in his ear, "You do such a great job of spoiling me, we might have to start our running routine early. That's okay in my book because we are on vacation and our plans involve French pastries. So, I'm good. Thank you so much."

I grab my clothes and run into the restroom to take a quick shower. Taking Logan's advice, I layer on several types of clothing. I'm sure I'll probably look like the Michelin man by the time I have my sweatshirts and coats on — but hopefully I won't freeze.

"I can't believe you're using your hat as a blindfold. So not fair. I can't even peek through this," I complain as Logan leads me down the beach. "I guess I'm not really upset because having a blindfold on makes me pay attention to what's going on around me. I don't remember so many birds yesterday and today, there seem to be a lot of kids around. I can hear them laugh and shriek and surprise as they run into the tide."

"I agree, there's lots of stuff going on today. I suppose we can thank the beautiful weather. Although, one thing you'll notice when you are in Oregon long enough is people here pay little attention to what's going on with the weather. They add more layers if it gets cold or windy."

"When I told one of my girlfriends I was moving to Oregon, she said no one here uses umbrellas. True?"

"Urban legend. People around here do use umbrellas — but maybe not as often as people from other states, because we are so used to the rain."

I shiver. "I'm not sure I want to get used to wet weather. On mornings like this I miss Florida."

"Well, depending on where you live in Oregon, you might not even have to. There are many areas of our state which don't get much water. Still, everybody assumes to live in Oregon you need to develop webbed feet."

I hold my hands out until Logan grabs them and rubs them to help me warm up. I snuggle up closer, and he gives me an embrace. "Can I ever take this blindfold off? I thought one of the biggest draws of the Oregon coast was its stunning beauty. I can't see the beauty through your hat."

Before Logan can answer me, something I hear makes my heart beat faster. "Oh my gosh! That was a horse. I heard a horse neigh!" It's all I can do not to squeal like a little kid. I know it would probably frighten the horse, so I try to contain myself.

"The cat is out of the bag now. You might as well take off your blindfold," Logan chuckles. "Meet Moon Star and Midnight. They will be our transportation on the beach today."

My mouth forms a surprised 'O' as I take off my blindfold. The horses are much bigger than I expected them to be. There is one which is a silvery-white color. I guess this one is Moon Star, as the other horse is pitch black.

I tug on Logan's sleeve to get his attention. "I suppose this would be an appropriate time for me to fess up. I love horses, and I read books and watch movies about them all the time. If I were independently wealthy, I would probably own several. However, the God's-honest truth is I haven't ridden one since I was a kid riding ponies at a birthday party."

"Oh wow! I must've misunderstood then. I thought you rode horses all the time back in Florida, just never on a beach."

"Nope, I wish. Will that make today impossible?" I ask as we walk up to the proprietor's equipment shack.

"I'm sorry, I couldn't help it. I overheard you talking about your experience as an equestrian," an older lady methodically puts a measuring tape around my forehead. She pulls a safety helmet from a shelf and hands it to me. She does the same for Logan. He is so tall, he has to bend down for her to be able to reach his head.

"I'm sorry, I don't have much experience — and what I have, I obtained a long time ago. I'll probably be useless on today's ride."

"Well, thank you for telling us. I'll put you on Moon Star. He is more experienced than Midnight. He is also smaller and easier to manage. Midnight is a big guy. He'll do fine with your boyfriend's dimensions."

"Are you sure we won't be interrupting the other customers? I'll need to go at a glacier pace."

"Don't worry about it. I will have my daughter be your escort. She's been on horses since she was two years old. There isn't anything she can't handle — even if you've never been on a horse before."

"I have a little more experience than that. Just not a

lot," I confess with a shrug.

"The real secret to being a good horsewoman is to respect your animal. If you respect them, they'll respect you back."

"Of course, I will be nice to Moon Star. This is like a dream come true." Turning to Logan, I practically bounce on the balls of my feet. "I can't believe you did this for me. It's one of the neatest things anyone has done for me in a long time. I'm so excited I can't stand it."

"I figured from the way you're dancing. I wish I had my video camera here."

"I think we'll all be happy you don't have it with you. No one needs to see what a fool I'm about to make of myself," I say with an embarrassed chuckle.

"I'm sure you'll do fine. Would you like me to help you up on your horse? I like to be gallant. It makes me feel like Prince Charming," Logan says with a grin.

"I don't know … you might have to lift me up and plop me on the horse. The stirrup looks like it's pretty far up in the air. It hits me at about waist-high."

"I'm here to help. You'll be surprised how quickly you get used to getting on and off a horse. The secret is to own the movement and try to do it all in one motion. If you're nervous, the horse will read that."

"I feel awful lying to Moon Star. I can try to fake it until I make it, but the bottom line is I really am nervous. I'm sure the horse already has gotten a clue. Don't you see him eyeing me?"

"I think he probably wonders if you have sugar cubes or carrots in your pocket," the lady in charge laughs. "He's a bit of a chow-hound."

"He and me both. It's a good thing he can't see how much I ate for breakfast, or he would probably go on strike."

The lady in charge rolls her eyes. "Oh come on! You're a tiny thing. I have people who ride my horses who are two or three times as big as you are and they don't have any issues. Are you ready to get started?" she asks as Logan and I walk over to the horse.

Before I put my foot in Logan's hands, I lean on his shoulders and say, "In case something terrible happens, I want you to know somewhere along the way, I discovered I'm in love with you."

I watch as a look of shock crosses his face. I bury my head in his shoulder as I try to cope with my embarrassment. Maybe I shouldn't have said anything. When I look back up, his lips are still pressed in a thin line and he hasn't uttered a word.

I want to disappear into some huge pit of sand right now. Sometimes, being blunt and straightforward may not be the best course of action. You'd think I would've learned by now.

Without acknowledging my statement, Logan says, "Careful now, it can be tricky to do this in the sand."

Much to my surprise, my muscle memory takes over and I'm able to get onto the horse without much drama. I wish that was true other areas of my life.

Chapter Sixteen

Logan

Katie is standing at my grill turning over chicken breasts. "Are we ever going to talk about what I said? I'm feeling weirded out that we haven't said a word about my tendency to blurt random things. What am I supposed to think?" She turns the burners grill off and moves the chicken to a plate. She strolls across the patio and sits down at the table on my deck. She takes a sip of her lemonade and continues, "The whole time we were riding horses, you never said a word. At first it didn't bother me too much. I figured I embarrassed us both. Then, I thought maybe you wanted more privacy. I've been petrified since you didn't say anything on the long drive home either. If I made a mistake by saying something, you have to let me know. I guess I don't understand what your boundaries are. The only thing I can figure is you must be royally pissed off at me."

Swallowing hard, I address the elephant in the room. "You could've knocked me off my feet with a feather. I did not expect you to take our relationship to that level quite so quickly. Now, I am at a loss of what to do."

She visibly bristles and her eyes light up with anger. "Gee, I'm sorry I put you into such a tailspin. I was just sharing my honest feelings."

"This is going to sound so cliché, but I mean it. Any reaction or lack thereof on my part is not your fault. I'm wired differently these days. Truthfully, I went into some sort of emotional panic attack when I heard those words. The strange thing is I feel the same way about you, but my past is keeping me from moving forward."

I hear Katie draw in a deep breath, but I can't bring myself to look at her yet. I need to get the rest of this out. I plunge ahead with my story, "This comes as a huge shock. I thought I had worked through everything there was to work through about Elyssa's death. I guess I was wrong because it's coming back to bite me at the most inconvenient time."

I glance over at Katie to see if I can figure out how all this is setting with her. Looking at her body language, with her arms crossed tightly across her waist and her nervous habit of cracking her knuckles, it's obvious this has not been a fun conversation for anyone.

When her expression grows stony, I try again. "I haven't actually told you this, but Elyssa was the last person I ever told I love you. After she died, I developed this fear that if I said the words out loud, the person I was talking to would also have something catastrophic happened to them. I didn't tell you about it because I was afraid you would think I'm nuts. Heck, some days I think I'm crazy. My paranoia is extreme. I don't even tell my family members I love them anymore. My mother is distraught, and my sisters hold it against me. I can't explain it to them either. My family never did understand my relationship with Elyssa. They kept waiting for us to outgrow our love for each other. Unfortunately, life had different plans, and Elyssa won't ever get the chance to grow up."

"That was incredibly unfair. I don't know why bad things happen to good people."

"If you ever figure it out, please let me know. It's a puzzle I've worked on for the better part of ten years. Honestly, I thought enough time had passed that I would be able to move on and love someone else. In my dreams, I always hoped to find someone exactly like you."

"So what's the problem?" she asks with a confused expression. "It sounds like both of us are at least on our way to falling in love with each other. I guess I'm lost."

"Unfortunately, it seems when push comes to shove, I have more issues than I thought I did. This is so stupid." I pace around the table. "I used to be a soldier — not only a soldier, but a soldier who fixed other broken soldiers. I've seen plenty of death. Why can't I put Elyssa's into perspective? It's not as if she was any more to blame for her accident than the soldiers who are hit by improvised explosive devices. This kind of stuff happens. I know in my head, but the rest of me hasn't caught up. I don't know if it ever will."

Katie walks right up and stops me in my tracks as she asks quietly, "Does this mean there is no hope? It doesn't matter if we've fallen in love with each other we have to try to put the genie back in the bottle?" She looks totally dejected as she walks over and takes a seat. She buries her head in her hands as she continues, "I'm not sure if I can voluntarily stop loving you because it makes you feel uncomfortable with your past." She wipes away tears with the back of her hand.

"That's not what I meant! I don't want us to call it quits. We need to figure out where our limitations are. I don't know if I'll ever be able to be a gushy guy who gives you presents and sends you text messages to say I love you. Saying the words out loud makes me break out in hives. I don't know how we reconcile what we need to happen in our relationship for it to thrive and my need to push my unhealthy flashbacks into the past."

For several moments, Katie stares at me. I wonder if I explained far too much. I've never told anyone else about my superstitious rituals. Only my family knows, which might be why I haven't spent a lot of time dating. I'm not exactly sure how to appropriately disclose my true level of weirdness. I look perfectly normal and functional on the outside, but the inside of me is a mess from my diabetes to my headaches and night terrors.

Life hasn't done me any favors when it comes to getting a healthy amount of sleep. If I'm not busy remembering Elyssa's accident, I'm reliving my shooting and all the soldiers who didn't make it. Some days, I put off sleeping because I don't want to deal with the horror of it all. I suppose I don't want to talk about it with Katie either because it makes me feel so helpless.

"I'm sorry, I have to disagree with your assessment of the situation," Katie says after an unbearably long amount of time.

"I beg your pardon?" I sputter. "Are you wearing my shoes?"

"I am not in your shoes, but I do occasionally steal your T-shirts to sleep in," Katie quips. "However, I can see what's going on in my own life."

"Go on," I instruct. "I can't wait to hear this." I raise my eyebrow in challenge.

Katie sighs. "Fine. You might disagree with my

assessment, but I think you have told me in several different ways since the moment you laid eyes on me you love me and care for me. Geez, Louise! Who rescues a drunk woman off the filthy floor of a dive joint and takes her to an award-winning bed-and-breakfast?"

"Technically, I wasn't the one who rescued you. Nick was."

"I heard the story differently, but it doesn't matter. Because Nick was apparently busy sawing logs during the two nights you stayed up with me to make sure I was okay. As I recall, he was nowhere to be found."

"He had a legitimate excuse. Aidan called them into work."

Katie flashes me a tight smile. "Before I met Aidan and Tara, I might have believed that argument. However, they are incredibly generous when it comes to leave requests. If Nick needed time off to take care of me, Aidan would've granted it in a heartbeat."

"You're probably right." He slowly nods his head yes. "Maybe the fact he chose to intervene had nothing to do with how attractive he found you." I sit down and scrub my hand down my face. "I think it has to do with him making amends for something he couldn't stop in his past."

"We all have triggers in our past which make us act differently than we otherwise would. I trust you to fight against those tendencies with everything you've got."

"I plan to. I didn't realize how much work I still have to do," I assure her, feeling discouraged at my lack of progress.

"We all have stuff to work on; don't sweat it," she instructs. "Anyway as I was saying, there virtually isn't any part of my life you haven't touched and made better. So if you can't ever say those words to me, having you do all the little things adds up to a much happier life for me."

"What do you mean? Are you talking about our relationship? From my perspective, I've done nothing extraordinary."

"Logan, where have you been? You stayed up all night nursing me when I wasn't even coherent enough to talk. Even so, you've been remarkably nonjudgmental over the whole deal. I'm sure you and Nick didn't expect to spend your vacation days being a nursemaid."

"Everyone has a bad day every once in a while. It would be strange for me to blame you."

"You've just made my point for me. If bad things are not my fault when they happen to me, why are you upset that you still struggle with Elyssa's death? In my book, that's silly."

"When you put it that way, I suppose it is. I keep thinking time will be the magical cure, but it hasn't been."

"I can't imagine the passage of time would ever be enough to have 'closure'. I know it's not the same exactly, but every time I see my brother, I can't help but think how much worse it could have been. It's been years since he lost his sight, but my mind automatically goes back to the time I saw him in the hospital with more tubes and wires than I could count. For several days, we didn't know if he would pull through his brain surgery to fix the aneurysm. But, he did and then we set off on the journey to see if he would ever get his eyesight back. Every time I have to wait for something as simple as a strep throat test, I flashback to the awful times we spent waiting to see if John was okay."

"Sounds hard. I suppose my family felt much the same when I was shot. They had to wait forever because I had to be flown to a couple of military hospitals overseas first before I ever got to the United States."

"I would like to sucker punch whatever clever psychologist or journalist or whoever came up with the term 'closure'. What a joke! There is no closure. I'm convinced it doesn't exist. I still have huge anxiety attacks if I so much as hear a car backfire."

"Really? I've been taking you to the gun range and you pretty much leave me in your dust. I would've never guessed you had any trouble with the noise," I say as I kiss her shoulder.

"If I'm in control of my environment, I can tamp down my fear. But when it sneaks up on me like a car backfiring or thunder and lightning, I am back on the hospital gurney begging for someone to call my parents and let them know what happened."

"I'm sorry," I remark, knowing how scary it is to get shot. Awkwardly, I try to change the focus of the conversation. "Speaking of semi-controlled environments, how do you feel about bad banquet food and dressing in sparkly clothes?"

Katie looks confused, but she nods her head. "Bad banquet food is not my favorite, but if you need me to go to somebody's wedding or something, I'll be happy to go."

"Actually, it's slightly bigger than a wedding, it's my high school reunion. It's time for me to go and face the music."

"Face the music? What do you mean?" She cracks her knuckles.

"Well, there are some people I graduated with who think I should have done more to save Elyssa. They think if they had been in my shoes, she wouldn't have died."

"Didn't you tell me she died of pneumonia while she was in the hospital, under the care of a doctor?"

I shrug. "I know. Even so, there are still certain people who aren't ready to forgive me yet. I can't let those people rule my life any longer. I've got lots of friends and supporters who were there for me after Elyssa's death. I need to go and check in on them. I want to make sure things are good and thank them for their support over the years."

"Makes perfect sense to me. I think you should go. I know it will be hard, but let's face it: you have been remarkably successful in your life. Your true friends will want that for you. They will be so proud of you."

"I don't know; I managed to get shot in what typically was a noncombat zone. But, whatever —"

"Yeah … and I managed to get shot during the service of a failure to appear warrant. Stuff happens. However, you didn't dwell on it. You've gone on to do really impressive things with your life. You are the head of security to one of the biggest pop stars around right now. You also protect a whole stable of singers coming up behind him. You are simply remarkable. You'll definitely win the 'I have the coolest job' contest."

For the first time this evening, I grin at Katie. "You know, you're right. I do have an awesome job. I'm proud of the fact I work for Aidan and Tara. He does great work and I'm proud to be part of his team."

"I know, right? So, how many days do I need to pack for?" Katie asks with an eager smile.

"Well, the reunion is a three-day extravaganza, but I figured I would spread out our visit a while longer so I can go see my family."

"M'kay, how many layers do I need to pack for this trip?" she quips with a wink.

"Not as many as for the beach. Didn't I mention we're going to Southern California? I grew up not far from Disneyland."

"Seriously? In all the time we've been together, I can't believe this is the first time you've seen fit to tell me. You and I need to have some serious dinner conversation. It would be fun to compare Disneyland to Disney World."

"It's been several years since I've even set foot on Disney property; I don't know if I'd have anything to contribute."

Katie takes a drink of her lemonade before she turns to me and announces, "I'll have to bring you up to speed. Disney properties are magical. It doesn't matter which coast you're on."

"I didn't realize how much I missed palm trees until this very moment. The trees in Oregon are nice, but they don't feel like home." Katie takes a deep breath of fresh air. "Can you believe I've never been to California before? Well, I guess you knew because you knew I had never been to Oregon either before I moved there. Sometimes I look at my life and think I'm totally nuts."

I place my arm around her waist as I maneuver my rolling suitcase with the other. "I hope you think I'm a good part of the crazy."

"Of course I do. I love you for all kinds of reasons,

but I won't deny being able to pick up and fly to another state on a whim is a nice perk of being together with you. It's not an extravagance I would do for myself."

I partially bow. "Why, thank you very much. It's not often I get to make a lady as beautiful as you happy."

Katie looks down at her ratty pants and oversized T-shirt. "I'm not seeing it today, so I suppose I'll have to take your word for it." As we walk to our rental car, Katie asks, "Where exactly are we headed?"

"Well, first we are headed to our hotel room to get cleaned up. Then we're going to dinner with my mother, Diya."

"This may seem like a dumb question, but why are we staying at a hotel instead of with your parents?"

"I wish it were that simple. My family politics have gotten complicated since my parents got a divorce. Rather than play favorites, it's easier to stay at a hotel. I love both of my parents and I'm sorry they can't get along. The funny thing is, they are both right and they are both wrong."

"Oh, I hate that. There is nothing worse than taking sides in an argument with your parents. No one comes out a winner."

"Well, in a way you'll come out a winner because my mom is making homemade *falafel* and *tabouleh*."

"Somehow, that sounds way more exotic than meatloaf and mashed potatoes. What if I don't like it?"

"I have a feeling you will. You like to experiment with food. Think of it as meatballs in a sandwich and a fancy refreshing salad. You'll be fine."

"Okay, as long as I don't have to pronounce it in

front of your mom. When I get nervous, I tend to stumble over my words. I have to tell you, I haven't been this nervous in a while. I might be reduced to a blubbering toad."

"Relax, it's my mom. She sells real estate, so she has a huge personality."

"What's your dad like?"

"Basically, he's the opposite of my mom. He designs medical equipment — you know those robots that are helping with orthopedic surgeries and such. My dad is shy, but he's got a wickedly funny sense of humor once you get to know him. Don't be surprised if he's reserved at first. He says it's because he spends so much time in the research lab he has forgotten how to interact with people."

"Hmm, must've made it hard for your parents. Sometimes opposites attract, but sometimes they just annoy each other."

"I think that's part of the reason my parents are no longer married. My dad is traditional and didn't want my mom to work outside of the house, but after we all had left home, my mom was feeling at loose ends. So, she went to some seminars and got licensed as a real estate professional and started a side business which has quickly grown. My mom is multilingual, and it helps her attract more clients."

"Multilingual? Oh no! I'm doomed to sound stupid. It's all I can do to communicate in English. Your mom does speak English, right?"

"Katie, you probably don't need to worry about it. It's been a while since I've seen my mom and she'll probably talk my ear off. In answer to your question: yes, my mom does speak English perfectly well. It is a popular language in Bihar. She also speaks Hindi and Bengali."

"Wait, do you speak all of these languages?" Katie asks as she furrows her brow.

I chuckle. "Only the bad words. As for the rest of it, I understand more than I can speak because mom and dad spoke other languages at home. However, they always encouraged us kids to speak English so we could assimilate better."

"Will your sisters be there?"

"It's not likely because school is in session right now. Sonia is studying engineering at Princeton University. Naina is studying psychology at the University of California and my sister Riya is a music major at the UCLA School of Music."

"If I was intimidated before, I'm petrified now. That's a lot of college."

"Yeah, that's one of the things you'll probably hear about this weekend. My parents are pretty disappointed I didn't take my EMT training any further. My dad wanted me to be an orthopedic surgeon."

"Do you have any interest in that?"

"Honestly, after my time in the hospital during my recovery, I was cured of all desire to do anything in the medical field."

"Is that why you don't do your EMT stuff as a civilian?"

"Primarily, but I'm also worried about putting my body under so much stress on a daily basis. As you've seen, the effects of my diabetes can hit randomly. When you're driving an ambulance, it might only be you and your partner. It would be dangerous to patients if I crashed and burned on the job."

"Isn't working for Aidan high-pressure?"

"Most of the time, working with Aidan is a study in administrative organization and tedious boredom. There are only a few times when it gets exciting. However, I always have backup waiting to step in behind me if something goes awry."

"I take it's why you added me to the team?"

"There are a lot of reasons I wanted you by my side. The job is only one," I admit as I reach out and grab her hand.

Katie takes a deep breath and lets it out. "Most of the time, I'm pretty fearless about being by your side — today I'm a mass of nerves."

"Don't worry, I've got your six. I swear you won't need me to protect you. My family isn't scary, just opinionated and smart. As nearly as I can tell, you'll fit right in."

CHAPTER SEVENTEEN

KATIE

I NERVOUSLY PACE IN front of the mirror as I wait for Logan to finish his shower. Last time I put this much effort into what I wore was my wedding day — and I know how that turned out. I hope all this preparation is not a bad omen.

Logan emerges from the bathroom wearing a pair of Levi's and a button-down shirt. I frown at my reflection in the mirror. I step away from the mirror and do a little spin in front of Logan. "Do you think this dress is okay? It doesn't show too much, does it?" I babble. "Should I wear a scarf over my hair?"

"Only if you really want to. My mom is not very traditional. My parents met when my mom was still a teenager after her parents fled to America. My mom has become thoroughly Americanized. She honors our cultural heritage, but doesn't push it on people. She doesn't even wear a sari unless it's a special occasion. My parents met and fell in love during a citizenship class. Even though my dad is more traditional, to hear my dad tell the story, it was love at first sight. It's funny, my mom tells an entirely different story."

"I don't know why I'm so nervous about this. Maybe it's because my relationship with Vincent's parents was so weird. At some point, I begin to wonder if it's me. I don't fit well into any one particular mold."

"I think that's precisely why my mom will love you. You are perfect."

I don't know why it surprises me that Diya looks like she could have stepped from the pages of a fashion magazine. Logan is tall and lanky and has an inherent sense of grace. It's all I can do not to stare at her because she is so compelling.

Diya embraces Logan. In a loud stage whisper, she comments, "I'm impressed, Logan. This one is beautiful."

"Thanks, Mom. I agree. Katie is beautiful from the inside out."

"It's nice to meet you, Katie," she says as she shakes my hand. "Truth be told, I was nervous to meet you. Logan talks about you all the time. I can tell you are important to my son. These days with the whole divorce rollercoaster, I can be a little much to handle. I don't want to scare you off."

I slump against Logan's side. "Oh good, I'm glad I'm not the only person who's jittery about today. These social situations make me anxious. I tend to be blunt and in-your-face; it doesn't always work very well for dinner conversation."

Diya looks up at Logan with a shocked expression, and my stomach drops to my toes and I want to cry. Is it possible I've already offended her with my greeting? I shouldn't be allowed in public, even with supervision.

To my surprise, she breaks out into a belly laugh. "Oh boy, are you in for it, my son. You've chosen someone remarkably like me. How is that for a karma-filled situation?"

"Mom, I've told you many times how I admire you. Does it really surprise you I chose someone with the same positive attitude and spunk you have?"

"I suppose not. You have always been a very smart boy. Although, your father would prefer it if you would go back to school and become a doctor."

Logan's sighs. "I know, Mom. I am well aware of his views. Dad has made no bones about his position on the matter. Can we not waste our time discussing the issue here? Katie and I are only here for a little while. I have to go to my ten-year class reunion. I'd rather not go into the situation feeling as if I've disappointed the universe."

"One more reason your dad and I are not together. I think our children should be able to choose whatever path they want in their lives. You seem happy on the path you are on. Especially now that Katie is in your life. I don't see any reason to change at this point. If you're happy protecting a musician, then you should."

Diya abruptly changes her focus to me and asks, "My son tells me you are in the same line of work. I am so impressed. It must've been hard for you to become a police officer. I don't know what it means in the grand scheme of the world, but I find it interesting that gunshot wounds have brought the two of you together to travel this journey."

I blush as I say, "I don't know if it was the gunshot wound so much as my very poor choices. I made a series of them before I met Logan. Frankly, your son is the best thing to ever happen to me."

" It's a funny thing. My son says the same about you. I may be skeptical about the power of love right now, but I can see you've been fantastic for my son. I haven't seen the lighthearted side of him in as long as I can remember. He seems a lot more like the little boy I raised, instead of a weary ex-soldier. He's told you about his military service, has he not?"

"Yes ma'am," I answer reflexively. "We've even compared our scars and our results at the shooting range. Even if I had planned to meet someone the day I met Logan, I could not have conjured up someone who was more perfect for me. He has been amazing every step of the way."

"Yes, I agree. Logan takes after me."

"Mom, don't ask her to take sides," Logan warns with a smirk and a glance over to me that says, 'I told you so'. "You know we're going to meet Dad this weekend too, and you know Katie has to stay neutral."

Diya reaches up and pinches him on the cheek as she says, "Oh, I know. But it doesn't hurt to recruit some girl power on my side. I miss your sisters, it's boring and lonely around here without them."

"I'm sorry, Mom. I know it's tough on you to have us all so far away," Logan says as he hugs his mom.

As I watch the interaction, I am overwhelmed by homesickness. Trying to put a lid on my emotions, I interject, "Look how well your kids are doing. You should be really proud."

"Yes, I am proud of my ability to raise four spectacular children. Despite what this one might tell you, I am equally proud of all my children."

I smile at Diya as I remark, "I have a hunch this weekend will be difficult for Logan, he needs all of us on his side."

"My goodness, *Beta* must have told you everything."

I look up at Logan with a helpless look on my face, hoping he will provide some clarity.

He catches my panicked glance and responds, "It's the Hindi word for son. My mom sometimes calls me that as a nickname since I am the only boy among three daughters."

"Yes, I've heard the story. It was very tragic … but that doesn't make it Logan's fault. I am afraid it'll take every ounce of my police training to keep my cool at the reunion if somebody lights into him and blames him for what happened."

Diya looks at Logan and announces, "I like this one. She reminds me of me. I have to warn you about something though. I was showing a house the other day, and Charlene Lippmann told me all about the reunion. I guess her daughter, Christalee, is on the planning committee. They are planning a big emotional tribute to Elyssa. Charlene mentioned to me she was glad you lived all the way in Oregon and wouldn't be at the reunion. Apparently, there are still some people who may give you a difficult time. I do not understand this — if the doctors could not save Elyssa, what makes people think you could have done more? You were just a high schooler."

"I don't know, Mom. I have turned that question over in my mind a million times. Now that I've been a medic, I wonder if maybe I could have prevented her from aspirating something that may have contributed to her pneumonia. I don't know. The fact still remains — I wasn't the drunk driver who killed her."

"Good question, why aren't they mad at him? He is the one who actually killed Elyssa, not Logan," I ask.

Diya moves her gaze between the two of us with a befuddled expression on her face. "How do you not know this? I figured someone would've told you by now."

"Know what?" Logan asks with trepidation.

"I guess you were away at basic training. Terrence Irving was let out on his own recognizance waiting for trial. I guess one deadly accident wasn't enough for him. Shortly before he was scheduled to go on trial for killing Elyssa, he got lit and drove down Laguna Canyon Road. The fool killed himself. I suppose I should be sad, but I'm not."

Diya abruptly turns toward me. "I hope it isn't hard on you for us to be discussing this. I don't mean to hurt your feelings, Katie — but, for a long time, Elyssa was the love of my son's life. She was like his other half. It broke my heart when she was ruthlessly killed, and people blamed Logan. Watching her die changed who my son was. For this reason, I'm not sad Terrence Irving died, but I am furious on behalf of Elyssa's family who didn't get the justice they deserved."

"If you are concerned that I don't know the importance of Elyssa in Logan's life, please don't be. It was one of the first things we talked about. On my more optimistic days, I'm happy she gave him his first lessons on how to be a great partner. On my more pessimistic days, I wonder if I'll ever measure up."

Logan puts his arm around my shoulder and hugs me close to him. "Katie, I'm sorry you feel that way, I wish there was something I could say or do. I can't change the fact Elyssa was my first love, but her existence doesn't make your love any less valuable to me. It's not about measuring up. Who knows? We were so young back in those days, we could have been like millions of other couples who drift apart and move on to other relationships. There is no guarantee we would've had our happily ever after even if she had lived."

"My son is correct, you know. In the beginning, I loved Tanish with everything I had. I gave him the best years of my life, and I was happy to do it. One day I woke up and noticed we had settled into being merely roommates. I deserve better. When I tried to talk it over with Tanish, he consistently denied there was an issue. Finally, I decided I was worth more. If he couldn't be torn away from his computer and drafting table, then what was the point of me being in our relationship? But, if you had asked me if we would end up in that spot when I was a teenager, I would've said you were crazy."

"You're not the only one. My brother went through something very similar with his former wife. When they first met, they had so much in common. As time went on and my brother was injured in the war, all the wheels fell off and John woke up and found out he wasn't married to the person he thought he was. It was sad to watch. But, now he's engaged to a phenomenal woman. Tayanita has made all the difference in the world to him. It's like I have the brother I remember from my childhood back. It's been great to see him rediscover himself."

"Yes! That's exactly what I'm doing right now," Diya exclaims enthusiastically. "I think I'm getting over the angry stage and figuring out who I am as a person again. It feels so liberating. I never knew how strong I could be without Tanish around."

"This is hard for me, Mom," Logan says in an unexpected moment of candor. "I understand how you feel because Dad tends to get wrapped up in his work, but I can't say for certain he did it to hurt you. I think he got used to you handling everything and swallowing your pain. I don't think he even saw it. The father I know would have done anything to make you happy. So, I don't know what happened — but it's hard to be stuck in the middle."

"I know. I shouldn't put you kids in the middle. I'm finally feeling better about what happened between us. Now that I have some perspective, I understand it's not all your father's fault. I wasn't listening to what he needed from me either."

"It sounds like there was plenty of pain to go around. It's always hard when things don't work out the way we expected. I think if I was in your shoes, I would feel much the same way Diya. It takes me a while to get over the anger."

"Yes, I can imagine it would. Logan told me all about your romantic problems back in Florida. I hope that jerk gets what he deserves."

I shrug my shoulders. "I hope so too, but the best

I can do right now is to try to forget the whole thing happened and move on with my life. I can't change who Vincent turned out to be. I can only move forward with my life. Fortunately for me, your son scraped me off the barroom floor when I tried to drown my troubles in Jack Daniels."

"So, you don't love this Vincent person, anymore? It sounds like he had quite the bankroll behind him. I know that can be tempting."

"Mom! Katie is not after anyone's money. Besides, I am very well-paid for in my position with Aidan; he takes good care of his employees. My bankroll is not suffering, if you know what I mean."

"You know, I understand your mom's question," I answer. Facing Diya I add, "But I wouldn't stay with the guy who treated me the way Vincent treated me for his money. I was willing to go it totally alone and walk away while my friends and family were sitting in the church. If I'm willing to take a stand there, I'm willing to take a stand anywhere."

Diya comes over and gives me a warm embrace as she says, "That's what I was hoping you would say. I want someone as devoted to my son as he is to you. By all appearances, you guys are both fiercely protective of each other and bonded as a couple. Honestly, after Elyssa died, I didn't know if he would find that kind of partnership again."

Diya's words make me catch my breath. "Thank you for your vote of confidence, I will do my best to be a phenomenal support system for Logan for as long as he wants me in his life."

"It's not a problem, darling," she says with a smile.

Logan pins a gaze on his mother as he says, "Mom, I think you missed your calling. With those interrogation skills, you should have been a law enforcement officer or an attorney."

"I'm sorry son, I needed to see if Katie here had the backbone to handle what life between the two of you can dish out. You guys have more than your fair share of struggles ahead of you. I want to make sure you know how to protect each other."

Something about her answer completely cracks me up and I start to laugh. "I should've been recording this conversation, because in a few years, you might not appreciate the fact I'm full of 'piss and vinegar', as my grandmother used to say. I'll warn you in advance, I can be very opinionated and mouthy. I might not be the respectful woman you think I am."

"No, I doubt it. I never got the impression you were terribly shy and reserved or even completely respectful. That's what makes our relationship fun because I'm the same way. Sometimes, I know the right thing to say or do, but there's this voice in the back of my head telling me I need to speak up and stand up for the right things. I have a feeling you are a lot like me."

I chuckle again as I respond, "Okay, so at least we're on the same page here. This is good. Now, do you mind if we go over the people who are likely to be at the reunion so I know who the players are?"

Diya glances over at Logan with a smug look on her face. "I'm already impressed with how brilliant your girlfriend is. Most people would not plan on a high school reunion needing a strategic battle plan. I love the fact she's thinking ahead."

Logan shifts uncomfortably on his feet as he says, "I know I should be glad, but the prospect of the two of you putting your heads together is more than scary to me. This could get interesting."

"Who wants a boring class reunion, anyway?" I remark with a wink.

CHAPTER EIGHTEEN

LOGAN

"Are you enjoying California, young lady?" my dad asks Katie as he sips his tea.

"I am. I was surprised how different Disneyland is from Disney World. It's much smaller. But, it was fascinating to think Walt Disney himself lived in an apartment right on the grounds. It must've been something back in the day."

"Yes, I suppose it was. I have engineering friends who worked on Twilight Zone Tower of Terror in the mid-nineties. They said it was a unique experience to work on a Disney project."

"I would imagine so," Katie smiles. "When I was little, I wanted to be a Disney princess, but it quickly became apparent I would never be tall enough. So, I changed my career goal, I decided I wanted to be an Imagineer. The only problem was I can't draw worth beans, and I have a terrible sense of spatial relationships."

My dad takes several moments to study Katie before he observes, "No, it is true you are not tall. You are not like my Diya. She is tall and strong like an oak tree."

"I met her the day before yesterday. Your wife is quite

lovely," Katie covers her mouth with her hand as she realizes her mistake.

"Don't worry, my dear. I consider her to be my wife for all eternity. It is a legal technicality we are no longer married. I will love her forever."

I have to swallow my groan. "Dad, have you ever told her? We were talking, and it seems Mom has a different opinion about how you feel about her. She thinks you are indifferent and fell out of love with her."

"If there is one thing I have never been with your mother, it is indifferent. She stirs my passion on so many levels. I thought she knew this."

"If I may say something … women are interesting creatures. We need to see evidence of how you feel about us before we believe it," Katie interjects.

"I honored my vows to my wife. I have provided her everything she could possibly need."

"No one is disputing your ability to support our family, Dad," I argue. "I think Mom feels like you don't support her ambition and passions."

"Ridiculous. One of my clients bought a house from your mother and repeatedly told me how excellent her service was. She even saved this client some money. He was so happy. I told Diya she did a good job, but she got offended by my compliments."

"Dad, did you leave it as 'You did a great job, Diya'? Or did you add your own personal philosophy behind it? Did you tell her she did a good job for a woman?"

Katie draws in a sharp breath as she waits for my father's answer.

"Well, I might have mentioned it is difficult for

women to succeed in business."

Katie sighs. "Yes, it is harder for us to succeed, but we don't want to be judged on a different scale than a man. We work very hard to compete in your world. We want to be acknowledged when we do a good job and not have it be diminished by the phrase 'for a woman'. That is probably why Diya was so upset."

"There is some logic to your statement. It was after that argument Diya decided she had outgrown our relationship and I would never change. I do wish to change. I just don't know what she needs from me. I never wanted to let her go. She is my other half. We've raised four children together. I thought the hard things were over," my dad says wistfully. "I thought we would be together forever."

"Dad, I am better at helping human bodies heal than I am at fixing relationships. However, it seems to me you and Mom need to have a serious relationship talk. Maybe you should even go see a counselor. I don't think your relationship is so far gone it could not be recovered."

"I don't know about counseling. Everyone just talks and talks and talks. Nothing gets accomplished. It is not like drafting. There is no concrete plan. It feels like a waste of time."

"With all due respect Mr. Anthony, if you love your wife, isn't it worth the time you spend to figure out what the problem is?" Katie asks with wide eyes. "After all, how often are the things you design as an engineer one hundred percent successful the first time you use them? Don't you have to go back to the drawing board and tweak the things which are not working? In my mind, counseling is not any different."

"Another solid point. I've never thought about it that way."

Before anything more can be said, my phone and Katie's phone simultaneously go off. We look at each other with a sense of foreboding. She is the first to reach her phone. She glances down at her text message and says, "Son of a biscuit! Not my house … I loved that little place." Tears well in her eyes.

With great trepidation, I take a call from Isaac Roguen. After I conclude my call, I address their questioning looks, "I'm sorry, Dad. There's been a change of plans. We need to return to Florida for a few days. I'm sorry we won't be able to go to the light show at Disney tonight. I need to get us on a plane as soon as possible."

"Is there anything I can do to assist, son?" my dad asks with great concern.

"Dad, I need you to work on figuring out what's going on with Mom. She may need your support through this. Katie has been attacked again. We don't know how far into her personal life this threat extends. Everyone connected to Katie could be in danger."

Katie leans forward and pins me with a serious gaze. "If so, I need to separate from you, my job and all of my family. I can't put up with some crazy person threatening everything and everybody I love. I won't give them power over me."

"I appreciate your efforts to shield people, but we are all trying to protect you too. The threat is primarily aimed at you. Like it or not, I am in your life now, and that goes for my family too. I'm not planning to leave anytime soon. You know this is hard for me to say out loud, but I need you to know this — I love you. I don't want anything to happen to you, so I'm not leaving your side — even if you think it's for the best."

Katie collapses against me in our booth. "I have waited what seems like forever for you to say those words and now I can't even celebrate our happiness. I have to figure out why my whole life is unraveling in front of me."

"I'm sorry, Katie. You should not have to face those kinds of threats from anyone. Rest assured, I know my son. He will take exceptional care of you."

With tears flowing down her face, she says, "I appreciate that, Mr. Anthony. I've known your son is someone I could rely on from the first moment I met him. I know he'll do his best to take care of me. On the other hand, Logan and I have both been on the wrong end of a gun before. Love does not stop bullets or fires — or wayward cars, for that matter. Logan and I have both been through enough to know we are not invincible."

"True. I worry about every single one of my children every day. Life is too short."

"Mr. Anthony, I really like you. I feel like we could talk for hours on end. Unfortunately, I can't right now. Still, I want to tell you love is fragile. So, if you have love in your life, you need to protect it with everything you've got."

My dad looks flummoxed. "You know, I am a very smart man. It doesn't take me much to figure out what you're talking about. I will take it under advisement. Maybe you and Logan will not have the only love story."

I get up and walk over to hug my father. "I hope not, Dad. I really hope for the best between you guys."

"The same is true for you, my son. Keep an eye on Katie and try to keep her safe. I have a feeling someday she might make a fine daughter-in-law."

"Dad, we have a long way to go between where we are now and thinking about something like that. Right now, we have to figure out how to save Katie's life."

"Well, when all the drama is over, I want to celebrate your love story. You have inspired me to try to rekindle my own."

"Mr. Anthony, my goal in coming to California was to help protect Logan. If I can help save someone's marriage, it's icing on the cake."

Katie is haphazardly throwing clothes into any suitcase she can. "I can't believe you got us a flight this quick. How in the world did you do that? It takes me longer to book a flight online."

"Sometimes, there is a perk of being both the bodyguard of a huge star and ex-military. I might've called in a few markers," I admit with a shrug.

"Whatever you did, well done! I just wish you could make the plane fly faster. Nine hours is a long time to wonder what the heck is going on."

"I hear you. Unfortunately, there is nothing I can do to make the trip less stressful for you. I wish I knew more about why they have summoned us back to Florida. Isaac was stoic about it. I suspect there is probably some huge development in your case he doesn't want to discuss over the phone."

"I can't believe this idiot attacked my home." She checks the drawers to see if she left anything behind. "I hate this! I was having a great time here with your family, and now I have to ruin all the warm, fuzzy feelings and face down some nameless faceless threat against me. This is not how I envisioned spending my time with you."

"Actually, I think you've done a great job this weekend. Everyone at the class reunion positively loved you. You stopped any of the naysayers with a single look. You gave me a glimpse of how you operated as a police officer and it was darn impressive. No one seemed to want to cross you."

"I think you might be biased by your past experiences," Katie answers. "My assessment of the situation as an outsider is you have a large group of core supporters, and then there are three detractors who were good friends of Elyssa's. They won't believe you regardless of what you say or do."

"I did notice. It is notable Clayton VanderHuson came over to my side. He used to be one of my biggest haters. Apparently medical school changed his opinion about whether I could actually have saved Elyssa. It was great to see him admit his mistake. Overall, I'm happy with the way things turned out. I feel vindicated now. I was never responsible for her death and it seems most people know. I accomplished my goals for this weekend. I am having an easier time putting the past behind me now."

"You know I don't want you to erase Elyssa from your memory, right? I know she was an important part of your life. The way I see it, she taught you how to love."

"Very generous of you, I don't know if I would feel the same way if you were mourning the death of an ex-boyfriend. I'd like to think I would be, but I don't know."

"I know the answer. I think you would find a way to be all right with it. You have learned a lot about being a decent human being from your parents."

I run my hand through my hair and check the time on my phone. "I think that was the biggest surprise of this weekend. If you would've asked me six months ago if I thought my parents could ever be on the edge of a reconciliation, I would've said you were crazy. But it seems like they've made a great deal of progress."

"I'm trying to be hopeful for them too, but I think it will happen in stops and starts. I don't think either one of them can completely reverse course. They have a lot of hurt feelings to work out between the two of them. However, I was encouraged your dad seems willing to try."

"Me too. I hope my mom is receptive to my dad's overtures. He's not the most romantic guy — he's kind of methodical and logical. I don't know if she'll recognize my dad's odd form of romance. It's rather understated at best."

"I wish your parents could've met my parents. My dad is the biggest mushy-marshmallow ever. Maybe I struggled to find the right guy because I was always trying to find someone who reminded me of my father. Do you know he puts a note in my mother's lunch every single day to tell her all the different ways he loves her? My mom has years and years of notes stuffed away in little commemorative jars — actually, no — *big* commemorative jars. My dad writes a lot of notes. She has them stored by year."

"Your mom kept them all?" I ask incredulously.

"Every single one from the first time they ever met."

"It looks like I have to step up my romance game too." I grin. "Do you suppose your dad would mind giving me some lessons?"

"No, I don't think he would mind at all. He knows every single communication style on the planet. He is like a little love evangelist. He teases my mom for being a matchmaker, but my dad is as bad as my mom."

"It sounds almost too perfect — your mom and dad are much different from my parents. They seem to be a lot alike. My parents are about as different as night and day."

"True, but my parents believe love can thrive in any environment."

"That's a good thing. I guess maybe between my years in the service and touring with Aidan, I have become a little jaded. Even Aidan and Tara who I consider to be my mentors are having some trouble."

"I don't know if they're having trouble between the two of them, it seems Tara is struggling so much with her loss they have started to talk past each other instead of to each other. Hopefully, time will help smooth over that situation."

"I hope so too. They are both great people — kind of like my parents. They're quite different, but obviously made for each other."

Katie takes one last look around the room as she collects her keys. "I guess it's time for this adventure to be over and go back to Florida and face the music."

Chapter Nineteen

Katie

WE'RE SITTING IN A conference room, which is suddenly stifling hot. It feels a bit like a greenhouse even though we are inside. I can't tell you how difficult it is for me not to be the one in charge of this meeting. It's as if I have no power over my own destiny right now. It is not a good feeling. I feel strangely demoralized.

We are waiting for the rest of the team to join Tristan and Isaac. They were kind enough to pick us up from the airport, but they refused to say anything until the rest of the team was present. Their joint silence is disconcerting and frustrating. Before this is all said and done, I might pull my hair out. I can't believe Isaac is being so closed-mouthed about this. I thought we had developed an off-the-books friendship when I was shot. He became like my honorary grandfather. The fact he is not talking at all freaks me out. The part of my brain that will always be a police officer is going absolutely nuts.

"They're late," I announce as I check the time on my cell phone. "How much longer do we have to wait for them before you tell me what is going on? Logan and I are tired, hungry, and sweaty. We would like nothing more than to crawl in bed and go to sleep."

Isaac smiles over at me. "You've had an exceptionally long day, but so have we. The rest of the team will be here shortly. Gareth Tanner stopped by to get more pictures made for you."

"Pictures? What pictures? Did you catch the jerk lighting my house on fire?"

Isaac pats me on the shoulder. "I know you have questions. But as I've already explained to you, I can't answer them without the whole team being here."

"I understand interview protocol and chain of custody, but I don't have to like it when I'm the victim. I have been waiting on pins and needles since the moment you called us while we were in California. I want to know what the heck is going on and why you needed us back in Florida."

The conference room door shuts quietly as Gareth walks in. "I think I can clear a few things up for you."

I look up at Gareth gratefully. "It's about time. What do you have for me?" I greet without preamble.

"It's nice to see you too, Officer Ashford," he responds pointedly.

"Tanner," I greet with a nod. "I'm sorry to cut to the chase, it's been a long day and I'm quite anxious to know what this is all about."

"I understand. Cody and I have been working closely with Tristan, Rogan and the rest of the team. We have come up with an identity or more precisely, we have eliminated a suspect."

"Oh good heavens, who did Vincent buy off now?"

Tristan laughs softly. "I understand why you would be paranoid. If I was your shoes, I might draw the same conclusion. However, Isaac and I are in on this investigation too. Trust me, unlike local law enforcement, I am not hurting for money. So, Vincent Hurlington can keep his own money."

"Great way to throw all of your old colleagues under the bus," Gareth adds with a frown.

"I apologize if it sounded like I cast aspersions on my former department or anything, I just know Vincent is an underhanded creep. He really wanted me to marry him. It seems he may be willing to pull out all the stops. There aren't many lines he would not cross if he thought it would benefit him."

"Understood. But, in this case, I think we were barking up the wrong tree," Gareth responds with a shrug.

Logan leans forward and grabs a legal pad off the table as he says, "What do you mean Tanner?"

"At first, we had an operating theory identifying Vincent Hurlington as the primary suspect — even if that designation was off the record. We had him under strict surveillance. The department doesn't have the resources, but several people volunteered."

I chew on my bottom lip as a horrible thought occurs to me. "Gareth, did Cody approve of these team members? You know some people on the force would rather see me suffer than succeed."

"Cody and I have been comparing notes. He has warned me of a few people to steer clear of, but he also told me who your biggest supporters were on the force. As it turns out, the people he identified as being your internal fan club at the police department were the first ones to volunteer their time off and skills to be able to surveil this creep for a while. I even got in on the hunt."

"Don't keep me in suspense — what did you find?" I press.

"The bottom line is even though your ex-fiancé's morals may be slippery when it comes to hunting down people's belongings from high-end robberies and installing their security systems, but he was not the person who lit your home on fire. It couldn't have been him. I was watching Vincent myself. I had eyeballs on him the whole shift. He was at some swanky party poking around the property. I was tracking him carefully to see if I could find something definitive to arrest him on."

"Can anyone else confirm this sighting?" I ask. "I'm sorry, but the guy's veins are filled with silicone, they're so slippery. He has big powerful attorneys on his payroll that could derail any case against him."

"If they try, they won't be very successful," Tristan answers firmly. "My team at Identity Bank can also confirm the visual. We were doing surveillance of the surveillance team because we weren't sure who was on your side and who wasn't."

I raise my eyebrow at Garrett's look of surprise. "You think I'm fighting against her, Macklin? What the heck are you thinking? Katie was one of the smartest people on our force. She had instincts well beyond her experience level. I wanted officers like her in our department. I would've gladly teamed up with her on the detective side of things. Her skills were wasted as a beat cop."

"I appreciate your ringing endorsement, but since I'm no longer with the department, it doesn't seem important to what's going on now."

"It's only important when you consider three people have now identified Vincent Hurlington as being at a different location than your catastrophic fire," Logan squeezes my hand.

I slump back in my seat as the ramifications sink in. "I've got two crazy people gunning for me? What did I do to offend the whole universe? Karma must be really mad at me."

"Since Vincent hasn't given up his negative vitriol against you, I am relatively certain your assessment is correct. In addition to Vincent's unpredictable behavior and ongoing campaign against you, I would say it is entirely possible he's still threatening you," Gareth answers.

"Don't forget, it could be one of the perpetrators you've already arrested," Tristan acknowledges.

"Oh joy! I don't think that's very likely because I wasn't with the police department long enough to gather any enemies. I think I only testified in a handful of cases. Why would anybody want to bother with me?" I ask as I abruptly stand up from my chair and start to pace around the room.

"We're not exactly sure. We're still breaking it down. However, it seems like the attacks against you are increasing in ferocity," Isaac observes.

"I agree. But this time, the joke is on the villain. Although the house is still my home of record, there was nothing left except for a few boxes of things for different charities that Ketki and Tayanita were planning to go through."

"Did she get them out in time?" Logan asks as he takes notes.

"I guess she got a couple boxes out before the fire. At least that's what she said in her text to me while we were in California. I don't know how much of it is true or if she was trying to calm me down," I explain.

"I know it seems like a total loss right now, Katie. But, it could've been so much worse. You could have been in your home and all of your belongings could have been in there and not on a freight train to Oregon." Isaac says as he takes a handkerchief out of his breast pocket and hands it to me.

I wipe away my angry tears. "I know, but it still pisses me off that my sense of privacy and safety were violated by someone who can't even be identified. You'll excuse me if I don't feel so lucky."

"The good news is Tristan and I may have identified a potential lead. We'll have to see if it pans out. That's why we brought you pictures."

Tristan lays out a few pictures on the table in front of where I was sitting. "Anything pique your interest?"

I walk back over and sit down as I study the photographs. They seem random. I gasp when I see the amount of damage to my home for the first time. "Oh my gosh! I'm sure glad Snoopy is staying over at Ketki's house. It would have been catastrophic if he had been there." I turn to Isaac. "Okay, I stand corrected. I am very lucky; I don't know if I would have escaped with my life if I had been there. You know me, I would've probably gone back to rescue my cat and been one of those victims we all hate to talk about."

I flip through to the later pages of the pictures, there are things I don't recognize strewn in my lawn. Puzzled, I hand the pictures back to Tristan who is sitting next to me. "I don't know what these are, they don't belong to my house."

"Are you sure? The appearance of these is slightly altered by the fire. They could look like something else entirely."

"No, I'm sure they are not mine. If I wear Hunter's Orange, I look sick. I prefer camo."

Tristan looks at Isaac. "It appears we may have confirmation of at least one of our theories."

Swallowing hard, I ask, "You think the perp was close enough to my house to leave these souvenirs behind?"

"Indeed," Isaac responds. "It seems our little firebug got injured by his own act."

"That is big news. I'm trying to remember at what point the DNA degrades so much you can no longer make a positive identification."

"Some of the stuff we found was well protected by other found objects."

"Would do you mean? There isn't a lot of stuff left in my house. Before I left, I took most of it with me, or boxed it up to give to one of the local charities."

"That's one of the reasons we don't think this is about the stuff left behind. It was too random for an arsonist to take the time to rifle through it. Not to mention he left your big painting untouched."

"Oh my gosh, I forgot I left it hanging on the wall. I planned to have Shelby or Savanna pack it up for me, but we got too busy."

"Your picture from Ketki is still in one piece. It didn't even get any smoke damage. Your case is so odd — it makes me wonder if this is the work of one individual or whether it is a group of kids. You know, like those flash mobs," Gareth explains.

"I suppose it's entirely possible. But the surrounding neighbors are all retired and home pretty much all day."

"We want you to take special notice of the pictures with property. We think he inadvertently dropped a few things in his haste to get away from the house. There is evidence he probably burned one of his appendages. There's some karma."

"Am I supposed to be sad this guy may have received what was coming to him from messing with my property?"

"I don't think any of us are suggesting that. We were hoping you could identify what was out of place in those pictures," Tristan points to the pictures on the table.

Taking my time to look through the pictures again, something catches my eye. "This looks like a welder's glove. See how it would go all the way to the elbow. On me, it would go all the way to my shoulder because I'm runty and short, as Cody likes to say. If that's a glove, it most definitely isn't mine." I turn to Isaac. "Was there DNA on it? Can't we put it in a super glue chamber to try to get fingerprints?" I ask.

Gareth nods at me. "Thanks to Isaac here, with his friends who are Feebies, we have samples on their way to Quantico. If anyone can unravel what's happening, they probably can."

"Don't you risk a jurisdictional fight? Wouldn't this be another law enforcement agency?" Logan asks astutely.

"We are not official or anything, but there are several of us working on your case who have formed an informal task force. So, at this point we are all working together."

Logan leans forward and looks Tristan directly in the eye. "I'm having a hard time believing with all the resources you guys have dedicated to this, you can't find who did this to Katie."

"Eventually, we will figure it out, but it will take some time and some mistakes on the perpetrator's side — like leaving items of clothing behind, for us to be able to make much concrete progress."

"I guess my real question is why did you fly me all the way to Florida to tell me my ex-fiancé likely did not do this and you have no idea who did this?" I press. "It doesn't make any sense to me."

"Honestly, we had hoped to make more progress than we did. But we wanted you here to make an ID on the perpetrator in case we could make a DNA match."

"But the DNA match only works if the person is already in the system — this could be anybody. You said so yourself. Aren't we back at square one if it's not Vincent?"

"You know how these go," Gareth cautions. "We can make a big leap forward on the case and then be stuck for a bit. An investigation can also pick up like a loaded freight train and speed up uncontrollably. We just don't know. Given Florida's unpredictable weather and the fact we are expecting some terrible storms tomorrow, we felt it was probably better to get you here today."

"I'm sorry, I don't mean to sound abrupt or rude, I'm extremely fatigued and jet-lagged. I was hoping you would have definitive answers for me. So, I'll visit with my parents and have a homemade meal with my brother and his fiancée. My dad would probably like to see Logan and me together. Our relationship status will probably be the happiest news my parents get all day."

Isaac looks at me. "I believe you're right. Thomas is a diehard romantic. He puts me to shame. In fact, after your mother showed off her wall of jars, I started writing my own notes to Rosa. I love to see her smile every single day. Right now, I think your dad is a relationship genius."

My stomach grumbles loudly. "Did I mention my mother cooks amazing food? I don't know if I am rooting for roast beef and mashed potatoes or macaroni and cheese. I am positive something she'll have will totally hit the spot."

Isaac and Tristan rise to their feet and shake my hand — I find this display of professionalism to be funny because my brother works for Tristan and Isaac has become like a cherished family friend, most of the time we hug. The formality feels a little strange. However, I understand them wanting to present a businesslike front to Gareth.

"Again, I'm sorry we've hit a snag in our progress, but hopefully it will be short-term and we will have some answers for you soon. Go enjoy being with your family and we'll be in touch," Isaac advises gently.

Shaking his hand, I say, "I haven't had much of a chance to tell you all how much I appreciate all of your hard work. Hopefully, we can unravel all of this and I can have peace of mind again and stop looking over my shoulder. I need the pieces of my life to make sense again, and I think catching whoever is tormenting me would be a good start."

"I probably shouldn't ask this," Logan interjects, "but I'm curious whether the surveillance teams have found anything nefarious about Vincent Hurlington's activities. I know a bunch of private eyes because I'm in the security business, but I don't know any who operate like Vinnie does. There must be more to his activities than meets the eye. I was hoping he would slip up when he was under surveillance."

Gareth grins at Logan. "Let's just say we're studying the tapes intently. I agree with you; I don't think merely looking into art theft and putting alarms in rich people's houses is enough to sustain a career — especially when no one's ever heard of you."

For the first time in a while, I smile a genuine smile as I say, "Tanner, wouldn't it be great if we get a two-for-one out of this investigation? I could live with that."

My former colleague regards me with a sad expression. "I always knew you were brilliant, Officer Ashford — great minds think alike. I hope we can get this done for you. We miss you in our neck of the woods."

CHAPTER TWENTY

LOGAN

I FIGURE SOMETHING GOOD MUST'VE happened on TV when I hear both John and Katie cheering in the living room. I don't think I've ever met bigger football fans than John and Tayanita. It's been interesting to see John in person, I've spoken to him over the phone many times, but seeing him cope with his visual impairment in person is a whole different experience. His dog Tuffy is contentedly ignoring the chaos around him and taking a nap.

Seeing Carolyn, I ask, "Is there a tray I should use for these drinks? I don't want to mark up your furniture."

"Oh, you don't have to do that, you are our guest," she insists as she takes the glasses from my hand.

"That's sweet of you, Mrs. Ashford, but I expect to be around for a while, you might not want to give me guest status yet."

Her eyes light up. "Are you saying what I think you're saying?"

"Not yet. We have lots of things to resolve in our lives before we can take such a big step. It is safe to say I love your daughter and I am definitely headed in that direction."

"Does she know this yet?" Carolyn asks as she puts her hand to her chest.

"I have made it clear to Katie I love her, the rest of it, we haven't had a chance to talk about much. I'm playing those cards close to my vest until things settle down. I don't want to upset Katie any more than she already is. Her last wedding was traumatic."

"You can say that again. My daughter had to run away from home because of that jerk. Don't think I'm not completely torqued over the actions of Mr. Hurlington."

As I'm speaking with Katie's mom, Ketki wanders into the kitchen. "I'm hungry, are we eating soon?"

Carolyn consults her kitchen timer. "We've got about a half an hour until the roast is finished. I made some fresh dinner rolls this afternoon; if you would like one to tide you over."

Ketki shrugs and says, "That's all right, I can wait half an hour." She turns toward me but looks over my shoulder as she asks "Are you Aunt Katie's boyfriend? Well, she isn't quite my aunt yet, but I call her that because her brother is engaged to my bio-mom, *Esti.*"

"I heard. Katie really likes you and your mom."

"I like her lots too. She likes to collect fun stuff, and she fights back against bad guys," Ketki says before she sighs heavily. "You know, Aunt Katie had a fiancé before, and he wasn't very nice. He called me names in front of a whole church full of people. I'm glad Aunt Katie didn't end up marrying him. He was a bully."

I smile at Ketki. "I'm glad she didn't marry Vincent either. I don't think it would've been a good match."

"Why do you believe you're a good match?" Ketki asks with a somber look.

"Interesting question. We have been dating for several months and no one has asked me that. I don't know if I can put it into words."

"Can you try? I'm trying to figure out why some people fall in love and other people don't. Figuring out relationships is hard for me."

"You know Ketki, I don't think it's easy for anybody to figure all this out. It's complicated, but I can try. There are a lot of things I like about Katie; she is smart and beautiful and funny. She is my biggest supporter. When I had to go talk to some people who were trying to bully me, your aunt stood up for me and defended me and it meant a lot to me."

"She is smart, but she's not as good at chess as John," Ketki comments.

"That might very well be true, but she has all sorts of great skills. Have you ever seen her in a dune buggy? She is like a professional X games competitor."

Ketki gyrates uncomfortably as a chill goes up her spine. "Thanks, but no thanks. I'll play my adventure games inside on the computer. Do you know sand gets everywhere? I can't stand it when it touches my skin."

"Gotcha. Next time Katie and I go to the beach, I'll try to get you some video of us riding sand buggies or maybe even a horse. She rode for the first time the other day."

"Sometimes, I wish I was as brave as Aunt Katie.

It's hard for me to do new things."

"I don't know. Katie was telling me about the story where you helped your Aunt Savanah. She said you worked directly with the Police Department. That was a brave thing to do."

"I don't know how brave it was; I was just helping them out with the computer games. I'm really good at computer games, so it wasn't hard. It's not like trying new things or meeting new people."

"From what I've heard, you did more than tinker around with a few computers, you were part of the investigation. Impressive."

Ketki shrugs. "I suppose if you say so. John says Katie is at risk. That's what my dad said too. Katie's cat Snoopy needed a place to live after Katie moved. Now I have two cat families. When I'm with Dad and Mom, we have Snoopy. When I go visit my *Etsi* and John, Corkscrew is my cat. John calls him a traitor because he was John's cat first, but he seems to have forgotten."

Ketki's habit of randomly changing the conversation in the middle has my head spinning as I answer, "Yeah, that sometimes happens. Animals decide who they want to be buddies with. Sometimes, what we want makes no difference."

"Do you have any animals?" Ketki inquires. "My Aunt Katie loves animals. She said before she was hurt, she wanted to be part of the K-9 unit."

I shake my head no as I respond, "Unfortunately, I don't have any animals right now because I am on the road a lot with Aidan and the other musicians. It wouldn't be fair for my dog have to have to stay behind."

"That's too bad," Ketki announces. "Everyone should have a pet. They are the coolest things ever."

I chuckle. "I'm not saying I disagree with you, I just am not in a position to have an animal at the moment."

"Do you mind if I ask some other questions?" Ketki asks politely.

I have to stifle a grin because she has been asking non-stop questions already.

"I'm all ears. Ask away."

"That's such a weird saying. English is dumb sometimes," Ketki frowns.

"I agree. My boss works with words all the time as a songwriter, he always tells me the same thing."

"Anyway, what I wanted to ask was if Aunt Katie will be safe? John was telling me someone has been doing awful things to her. He's worried about me too. He was upset when Katie's house was burned down to the ground. He was afraid that Tayanita and I almost got caught in the fire."

"Oh, I didn't realize you guys where there so close to the time the incident happened."

Ketki shoots me a small smile. "No, we weren't. But John is super protective of both of us. I think he was being a worrywart, but I don't know. So, that's why I'm asking you."

"Ketki, you are old enough to understand there are truly bad people in this world. Someone has decided they don't much like Katie. I don't know what their issue is or what they hope to accomplish, but it's not a good thing."

"But, it's good Tristan and Isaac are helping with

the police, right?"

"I think it will be really helpful. Isaac and Tristan know a lot of talented law enforcement officers. So, they can help your aunt's former unit track down whoever is doing this to her."

"So, after you find the bad guy, are you moving back to Florida? I think everybody misses Katie."

"Honestly, we haven't figured it out beyond coping day-to-day with whatever challenges are thrown in our face."

"But your job is in Oregon —"

"I know. That's what makes it hard. But we'll try to visit as often as possible if we do end up in Oregon."

"How long are you here this time?"

"A lot of that will depend on what the police department needs Katie to do. But, at this point we are scheduled to leave next Wednesday."

"That's not much time," Ketki comments mysteriously.

"Time for what?" I ask when I see the odd expression on Ketki's face.

"I have more plans to make, I can't talk about it right now. But I'll let you know later."

"Oh, okay —" I respond.

"Hey, Logan are you ever bringing those drinks? We are dying of thirst in here. Being an active spectator of sports is hard work," Katie asks.

"Coming! I got a little distracted," I answer as I stack the tray with beverages and snacks.

"You're busy right now, but can I have your cell

number so I can text it if I have questions? I am really worried about Aunt Katie."

"Sure thing. Remind me to give it to you later after dinner," I offer.

"Thank you for talking to me, I feel much better," Ketki says as she skips out of the room.

After she leaves, Carolyn taps on my shoulder. I wasn't even aware she was still in the room. After I slow my racing heart, I ask, "Can I get you something to drink too?"

"Oh no, I'll just sit down and do some cross-stitch. I am not a huge football fan. But, I wanted to tell you I'm so glad you are looking after my daughter. It means the world to me."

"Are you ready for this?" Katie asks as she nervously twists her fingers in her hair.

"To tell you the truth, I don't know. I have no idea what we are walking into." I look over at Katie as we wait for the stop light to turn green.

"Don't you think it's strange they're calling a meeting at nine thirty at night?"

"It's hard to say, they might just be trying to accommodate our limited time in Florida."

"It's weird, I thought I knew what this process felt like having been a police officer, but it's completely different when you're on this side of the table. I have a better appreciation for how nervous people were when they came to the police station — even if they weren't suspects."

"I had a similar experience after I was shot. I had enough medical knowledge to scare the crap out of myself, but I had very little experience being a patient."

"Isn't that the truth? Ask John, he'll tell you I made the world's worst patient."

"I don't think either one of us can be described as having a laid-back personality, so, it does not surprise me. Once an adrenaline junkie, always one — at least that's what I think."

"Well, right now I have too much adrenaline in my system. I could do with less excitement in my life. Having a target on my back is not fun."

I pull the rental SUV into a parking spot at the Sheriff's office. I walk around the rig and help Katie out. As I lift her from her seat, I pull her into a quick embrace. "Whatever we find out today, we will make it okay. I promise."

Katie sighs. "I know you would like that to be true, but you and I both know wishing things are fine doesn't actually make them fine."

"It's probably wishful thinking, but maybe they have figured all of this out, and this nightmare will be over."

Katie slides her arm around my waist as we walk into the building. Before I have a chance to knock on the door of the conference room, she leans up and kisses the bottom of my jaw as she says, "You don't know how much I hope you're right. I just want to get on with living my life with you."

"Me too," I comment as Isaac swings the door open.

"Oh good, everyone is here now." He gestures toward the table of people waiting.

I grimace. "Sorry, we didn't realize we were holding up the meeting."

"No problem, we were just reviewing the files before we called you. We realize you had to come from across town."

"I'm sure a lot of people would want to ease into this conversation, but I want to know why we are having a late-night meeting. Is there something new?" Katie asks impatiently.

Gareth looks up at Katie. "Yes, we have a potentially solid lead. We don't have all the details yet, but it gives us a direction to go in."

Katie and I rush over to the table to sit down. "Maybe this is the break we've been waiting for." I pull the file I've gathered out of my backpack and set it on the table.

"Mr. Anthony, I've added you to the law enforcement task force because you are providing personal protection for Ms. Ashford. By doing so, I can read you in on what's going on," Gareth informs me with a grim expression.

I breathe a sigh of relief. "When I filed for all the paperwork with the International Association of Bodyguards, I wondered if it would be worth all the hassle. I figured there might be some potential professional development opportunities I could use to help keep the folks at Silent Beats safe. Now I'm glad I completed all the coursework for certification."

Tristan nods. "We are too. If we're ever questioned, we can point to those."

Katie practically growls with frustration. "I know Logan is qualified, I've known from the very first moment I met him. He is a good guy through and through. So, can we get on with why we're here?"

Gareth raises an eyebrow. "I can see life on the West Coast hasn't mellowed you out any. You are still one of the most driven people I've ever seen."

Katie twists the ends of her hair in her fingers as she says, "Okay, I plead guilty to being intense about this. But it's affecting my whole life. My future niece is completely freaked out. I would like to get it resolved and behind me so we can all go back to our regular lives."

Gareth pulls out a stack of photos and shows them to Katie one by one.

"You know the drill — if you see someone who looks familiar, let me know. The suspect may or may not be in this group of photographs."

Katie's face lights up. "Oh my Gosh, they must've gotten some DNA back from Quantico."

"Affirmative," Gareth nods tightly. "We need to know if any of these look at all familiar to you."

Katie pulls her reading glasses out of her purse and studies the pictures as Gareth presents them. I have a knot in my stomach because this is a crucial step. If Katie can identify her attacker, it will be huge.

Katie asks to go through the pile of pictures three times. Finally, her eyes tear up. "I'm so sorry, but I don't recognize anyone in this stack of pictures. The closest thing is the blond guy with the beard but only because he looks like he belongs in a toothpaste ad or something in my Facebook feed. I don't think I personally know him."

Isaac comes over to comfort Katie. He lays his hand on her shoulder as he says, "Remember, we never said his picture was in the group. Don't worry about it, you did your best."

"That's not good enough for me, Isaac. I need to know what's going on. This cat-and-mouse game is driving me crazy. I can't relax and focus on my new job because I'm worried about what's happening back here at home. This has to end at some point."

"I know it has to be incredibly frustrating, but we're working on it. We've discovered a familial link between the glove left at your home and Kirk Coggins."

"The guy I shot?" Katie covers her mouth in shock.

"But the shooting was justified," I add. "He shot her first."

"I understand, but apparently, Mr. Coggin's family does not."

"Do you suspect the mother and father, or a sibling?"

"At this point, we know the suspect is male, so that eliminates the mother. The mother and father are professors at Oxford University, so they are not considered suspects."

"Wait a second … the guy I shot while I was serving a failure to appear on a domestic violence charge is the son of college professors?"

Isaac nods. "Creeps come from all demographic backgrounds."

Katie shakes her head. "I guess my life at this point is a case study in breaking all the stereotypes about who the bad guys should be. I mean, I know you don't necessarily have to come from a bad neighborhood or have a bad family life to turn out to be a colossal freak, but this is ridiculous."

"Katie has a good point. Is there any evidence the

Coggins' know Vincent Hurlington? They may travel in the same circles," I ask, before I take a drink of my now cold coffee.

"We're still investigating. But at this point, we have found no connection." Isaac looks over at Gareth as he says, "Even though she hasn't identified him, should we show her his picture so they know who to watch out for?"

Gareth nods. "I think that would be the most prudent course of action given the circumstances. I want to make sure Katie has as much information as possible to keep herself safe."

Gareth shuffles through the pile and pulls out a picture.

"It's the toothpaste guy!" Katie cries. "I thought he looked shifty."

"So, where is this guy now? Do you guys have eyes on him?"

"Not yet. But, we're working on it. Mr. Coggin's is a software marketer. He travels a lot. At the moment, he is out of state."

"So, what should I do? Sit around and wait to see if he strikes again?" Katie asks tensely.

"You are only here for a few more days, correct?" Gareth confirms.

I nod. "Yes, we are scheduled to take a flight out early Wednesday morning."

"We've got enough manpower right now to help you watch Katie's back while you're still in Florida. However, I would recommend you stay on the West Coast for a while."

"You have no idea how much I wish I was on the

other side of this desk. Being a crime victim is the pits," Katie declares with a fierce look.

"Hopefully, this is enough information for them to get him off the streets. I know it doesn't seem like it right now, but I think this is a positive development because at least now, you have a name and a face and a reason. We're not just chasing the boogie man anymore."

Katie rolls her shoulder. "I suppose you're right. But, the fact this is personal and not just generic violence against me as a police officer, makes it even more terrifying."

"I'll do my best to make sure this guy is stopped," I vow.

"I had no doubt, I trust you implicitly — it's the rest of the world I'm unsure about," Katie replies with a teary smile.

CHAPTER TWENTY-ONE

KATIE

"I can't believe how domesticated you've become. You're going to give Mom a run for her money when it comes to cooking." I watch my brother make a roux for homemade macaroni and cheese. "I'm still trying to figure out how you don't burn it. I can see perfectly fine, and I still mess up."

John points to a timer around his neck and then his nose. "Between the two of these, my cooking has become much more precise. Cooking is all about patience, you have to take your time to do each step."

I roll my eyes at my brother. "Hello? How long have you known me? I am not very good at waiting around for things to happen."

"Speaking of which, have there been any developments in your case?"

"No, not as far as I know. No one has updated me. I don't suppose you know? You know … because you work for Tristan."

"Sorry, Sis. I work in an entirely different section of Identity Bank."

"Well, that's not helpful," I tease.

"Hey, I'm only the big brother. I'm not God. I can't be helpful all the time," John says with a grin. "Since you're here and everything, how would you like to help me with a secret project?"

I practically dance with glee. "Yes, please give me something to do. Waiting for something to happen with the investigation is driving me absolutely crazy. It's worse than watching grass grow."

"Okay, you're in. Hopefully, we can pull this off."

"Ohh, I haven't done anything undercover in a while. This is exciting. What are we doing?"

"Planning an understated wedding —"

"Ha, ha! You're funny. You have met our parents, right?"

"No, I'm serious — Tayanita and I got our marriage license a few weeks ago."

"Shut up! Why didn't you tell me?"

"I didn't know if we'd be able to pull it off. It was kind of a spur of the moment thing. Tayanita says she doesn't want to make too big of a deal of it because it's not like I can enjoy the pictures of our wedding."

"Well, you can't, but the rest of us can," I sputter.

"I thought so too. She planned to have a friend who's attending Bible school at night officiate for us."

"I don't know, John. It seems risky to throw a surprise wedding. You could upset a lot of people. How much does Tayanita know?"

"Tayanita is in the middle of a federal review of the hospital right now. She has all sorts of reports to write. She finally threw up her hands and told me if I wanted something more than a simple ceremony I should plan it myself. I think I'll take her up on that."

"You know, I have a reputation for being the wild and crazy child with an impulsive streak, but I don't know, this sounds downright insane. Does Tayanita even have a dress? Wedding dresses take time."

"Somehow, she's got a dress — although she won't tell me how all of it came about. So we're good there."

"You silly, silly man." I giggle. "Don't you know women have crazy superstitions when it comes to guys knowing about their wedding dresses?"

My brother shrugs. "Whatever. It's clothes. I'm not marrying her for the dress."

"True. But the dress is part of the whole ritual — or in my case, something I want to burn. I can't believe I'll be paying it off forever."

"I expect you might be making more money working for Aidan than you were as a public servant. Am I right?"

"Says the guy who is working for a software titan," I counter.

John takes a bite of macaroni. "Do you mind draining the water for me?"

I pick up some hot pads and drain the hot water into the sink. "Got nothing to say to that, do you?" I tease.

"Actually, I have a lot to say. For all the weird circumstances which brought me to this point, you and I are both exceptionally lucky people. We are like cats with nine lives able to land on our feet."

"Not a day goes by I don't think something similar. I can't believe I found the love of my life a few minutes after the biggest debacle I've ever had. There's something screwy about that kind of fate."

"You're lucky he stayed around, I've been around you when you're toasted. You tend to be mouthy and rude. So, Logan must have the patience of a saint."

I think about his assertion for a moment. "I wouldn't call Logan patient. Strategic, maybe, and one of the kindest people I've ever met. Patient, not so much. The two of us are driving each other crazy with all this waiting. Please make sure you give Logan a role to play in this wedding so he can get his mind off my troubles. He is so worried he's not even sleeping well."

"Well, there's plenty to do. We don't have food, entertainment or anything."

"Do you have a venue yet?" I ask.

"We do. One of Tristan's friends has built a wedding venue on his horse ranch. I thought since Tayanita and I like to spend so much time outside, it would be a sweet tribute to how we bonded."

"What a great touch! You don't know this, but I've become a pretty good horse woman. Don't worry about the entertainment, Logan can handle it. He is connected up the yin-yang. So, he should be able to find something for you."

"Spectacular idea. It makes perfect sense."

"I've got one more question. Is Ketki in on Operation Rapid Wedding?"

John shoots me an amused grin. "She is. I clued her in the other day and she is so excited she is about to bust her buttons."

"How are you managing that? Ketki isn't very circumspect when it comes to the things she comments on."

"I don't know how long this will hold, but so far she is toeing the line. She has been waiting for us to get married for a while. She doesn't want to do anything to blow it for me. She actually makes a good partner in crime. She is so smart. If one of the software giants don't snap her up before she even goes to college, I would be surprised."

"You would be surprised how often I hear similar comments about your soon-to-be stepdaughter. It seems like she is gifted in a lot of areas. Savannah still brags about how instrumental Ketki was in helping to catch her tormentors."

"As she should; it was an impressive takedown."

"What is Ketki doing for this event?"

"I believe Ketki is working with Rogue to come up with the bridal party and dress them appropriately."

"You're telling me everyone knows about this except for Mom and Dad? That ought to be interesting. I don't know how Mom will feel about being left out of the loop."

"Tayanita and I will eventually add them to the loop. But we want to get things set before Mom tries to take over. She tries to be helpful, but it can be overwhelming and since Tayanita is in the middle of her huge work project, it was too much to deal with."

"I understand. Remember, I went wedding cake shopping with Mom. She about drove the bakery to tears."

John shrugs. "I guess Mom means well. But she's a little too enthusiastic."

"Hey, don't knock the enthusiasm, sometimes it's all we have. You're lucky I haven't spontaneously burst out into a bunch of eighties love songs. Even though it's very risky, I still think it's a wonderful surprise. I think Tayanita will be pleasantly surprised. She doesn't like to ask for a lot for herself, so the fact you're doing this on your own will mean a lot to her."

"I hope so. It would be terrible if the surprise went sideways."

"Well, we just have to make sure it doesn't."

I straighten Logan's tie and try to smooth out the wrinkles in my dress. "Wow, it's hard to imagine I've already become acclimated to Oregon, it feels stifling hot here. Before I moved to the Northwest, I didn't even notice it."

Logan fiddles with his cufflinks. "I agree, it's sticky out here. What a great place, though; I love the free-range horses. Maybe my friends, Madison and Trevor, should do this with their little farm."

"It is beautiful here, I love all the different venues."

"It's too bad John can't see them because they are breathtaking," Logan comments.

"Have you been listening to Tayanita talk to John today? She is providing the most comprehensive descriptions you can imagine. I'm sure my brother can see every single detail in his mind. I've often wondered how they cope with their nature hikes, but now I understand. They are like the perfect team."

"I haven't known either of them for very long, but I think they're cool."

"Thank you so much for getting the entertainment for today. I think it's great Declan was available to sing. It was thoughtful of him to have Joe Summers come along. It'll be like our own private concert."

"I've been watching Joe Summers in rehearsals. His ability to sing a ballad is remarkable. It will break your heart into a million pieces."

"You know, Tayanita won't be happy. It's hard enough to wear makeup without it washing off because of our tears."

Logan pulls me closer and kisses me. "I guess that's the risk you all have to take. Trust me, this guy is worth it."

"I can't believe Ketki convinced Walter to do the ceremony on such short notice. I remember him from Shelby's wedding. He is great."

"This time, I think it was timing. Walter and Wilma happened to be here visiting. I love the way this all came together even though it could have been one big train wreck."

I playfully swat him in the arm. "Shush! You can't say things like that. It's like daring the universe to make something go wrong."

Logan chuckles. "Yeah, we had the same concept when I worked as a field medic. No one was ever allowed to say the word quiet. The minute someone mentioned a lull, something huge would always erupt."

"Exactly! I need to check in and see if everyone is ready for pictures." I examine myself in the mirror and then do a little twirl in front of him. "So, what do you think? Do I look ready to get a new sister-in-law?"

"In my book, you're pretty much perfect every day. But you look exquisite today."

"Thank you very much. You look handsome too."

Our conversation is interrupted by a knock on the door. Ketki sticks her head in and whispers, "Aunt Kate, I need you quick."

Immediately, Logan's body language tenses. "Is there anything you need my help with?"

Ketki shakes her head. "No, it's a different kind of emergency. I don't need a bodyguard; this is a girl thing."

I quickly stick one more bobby pin in my hair as I say to Logan, "I guess I'll be back. If not, save a chair for me."

Ketki practically drags me down the hall as she says, "Aunt Kate, I don't know what's going on with *Etsi*. She is having a major freak out and ruining all her beautiful makeup. I'm afraid she'll get her dress dirty."

"What happened?"

"I don't know. I was putting on my shoes. I didn't see. I guess your mom brought in a box for my mom and the next thing I know, *Etsi* was crying like she had a sliver. But then, it seemed like once she started, she couldn't stop. It's kind of scary."

"Ketki, take a deep breath. I'm sure it'll be fine. During my wedding, I had a meltdown when I had to stop in the middle of getting ready to go to the bathroom. So, these things happen. I'm sure everything is okay."

"It doesn't feel like it's going to be okay. My mom never gets like this."

"I know Sweetie, but weddings bring out strange things in people."

"I heard John tell somebody you met Logan when you were drunk off your butt in a bar. Is that what you're talking about?"

"It definitely covers things like that. But I don't think whatever's going on with your mom is quite as serious. I bet she's just stressed and tired."

When we hit the doorway to the little room off the ceremony space, I see what Ketki is talking about. Tayanita is a mess. I haven't hung around with her a lot, but in the time I've known her, I've never seen her undone like this.

I walk over to one of the end tables next to the couches and grab a Kleenex before I hand it to her. "What's up Tayanita?" I ask, as she blows her nose.

Tayanita glances up at me with surprise. "Oh, hi. Don't mind me, I'm just overwhelmed right now. Do you know how much your brother loves me?"

"Tayanita, I hate to break it to you, but anyone watching the two of you totally knows that. It's not a secret."

"Yeah, I know but he loves me a lot. This wedding is beyond anything I could've imagined. You know, I thought I blew my chance at the perfect wedding when Mark and I didn't work out. I mean, our wedding was pretty, and my parents really tried hard, but it wasn't anything like I wanted. But, this is different! It's like John crawled right in my head and pulled out all my ideas to make this perfect."

Tayanita pulls up the skirt of her beautiful Grecian-style gown and shows me her feet. "Look, I even get to marry my husband in my bare feet. I told him when we first met if he didn't approve of bare feet, he didn't need to fall in love with me because I spend every waking moment I possibly can without shoes on. He honored the request."

"I am not surprised. John has a knack for hearing the things people don't say as well as what they do." I look in the mirror and straighten my hair. "So, my big brother loves you a bunch, why are you sad?"

Tayanita holds up her wrist and shows me a delicate silver charm bracelet. "Look at these charms. They cover all the things that make me ... well, me —" she breaks off with a helpless shrug. "He sees all of me and loves me anyway. What if I don't deserve any of it?"

I reach up and give my soon-to-be sister-in-law a hug as I say, "You deserve it. All of it. The decisions you made with Ketki and Mark are behind you now, and they were never really you. The effects of postpartum depression were driving your choices. You are not in that place now. Go celebrate."

"Do you think it is possible for love to triumph over evil?" Tayanita asks me tearfully.

"I believe it with my whole heart. I see evidence of it every day," I assure her with one last hug. "You can do this. You have taken so many leaps of faith — you can take one more into happiness."

Logan walks up behind me and cuddles me to his chest as he murmurs in my ear, "How are you doing? Are you hanging in there?"

"My hairstyle isn't holding up very well, but my heart is fine. I thought this would be harder, but I can tell the difference between Vincent's showboat of an extravaganza and real love. This underscores the fact I made the right decision to walk away," I respond as I relax against him. "My brother looks so happy."

"I totally agree. Aidan used to play a lot of weddings back in the day, and this is one of the most romantic ones I've ever seen."

"I thought Ketki did a remarkable job. It was incredibly sweet for her to be a narrator for John so he could envision how lovely Tayanita looked coming up the aisle. John was a complete mess. I am totally impressed with how he and Ketki have bonded. It is an atypical family, but it's a family nonetheless."

"I thought it was very classy of Mark and Shelby to escort Tayanita up the aisle since her parents couldn't make it on such short notice," Logan adds. "I am so glad I got to meet all of your friends and family."

"Do you ever get the feeling my friends and your friends would completely jam? If we ever do this, our wedding will be epic."

"I've often thought the same thing. I wasn't sure if you would put yourself out there again. I don't want to put any pressure on you."

"Several months ago I would've said it was unbearable pressure, but now I can't envision my life without you in it. My perspective has completely changed. We just have to catch a few bad guys first."

Logan gives me an amused smirk. "Did we just ask each other to get married?"

I let out a startled burst of laughter. "You know, I think we did. So, what's your answer?"

Logan kisses me soundly as he says, "My answer today, tomorrow, or next year is an unequivocal yes."

"Oh good, I would hate to think we weren't on the

same page. Logan Anthony, a man of two first names, I would love to become Katie Anthony. I love you so much. Thank you for saving me from myself."

"You might think I saved you, but in many ways, you saved me. I have never been this happy."

I frown. "Now that we are unofficially, officially engaged, where do we go from here?"

"Long term, we have to do some planning, but short-term, I would suggest we hit the dance floor."

"Sounds like a reasonable strategy," I say as I grab his hand and walk into the middle of the dance floor. At the moment, Joe Summers is singing *Unanswered Prayers* by Garth Brooks, and I can't think of a more appropriate song.

Logan pulls me close and places his hands around my waist as we dance. He leans down and murmurs in my ear, "Are you thinking what I'm thinking?"

I nod. "There's nothing like song lyrics that speak to you personally."

"I am so glad Nick encouraged me to be a hero on a day I didn't feel like being one. Meeting you is the best thing that's ever happened to me."

Chapter Twenty-Two

Logan

AIDAN IS HAVING ONE of his famous jam sessions with his crew when Katie and I walk through the door. As soon as we enter the room, the whole place bursts out in applause.

Katie blushes a deep shade of red. "What's this for?"

Stella, Aidan's backup singer, answers with a grin, "Well, it's not every day we send somebody on a mission to catch a bad guy, and they catch the best guy around."

"Well, it wasn't just me. We became mutually engaged," Katie answers with a chuckle.

Tasha looks up from her guitar. "I think we need more details."

"It's pretty simple. We both had a great idea at the same time and asked each other to get married," I answer with a puzzled look. "Come to think of it, how did you guys find out? We didn't go public on social media or anything."

"Well, it turns out Tristan is a huge believer in love at first sight. He finds your story fascinating. So, he might've spilled the beans."

"I don't know … I smell my brother's hand in this, too. He was sad I didn't announce our engagement at his wedding because we didn't want to take away his limelight. He wanted to throw a big shindig for me, but didn't get a chance because they went on their honeymoon."

Aidan looks down at the ground. "Okay, so there might've been a mention of a grand celebration to be scheduled shortly."

I cringe as I address my friends, "You know I'm not big on the public stuff. I'm more of a behind-the-scenes kind of guy."

"Now, Logan you've been my friend long enough to know you won't get away with that. An unexpected love story is always cause for a party."

"I know, that's why it scares me. You and your gang are famous for throwing surprise weddings. I'm not sure I trust you guys."

"Oh come on!" Aidan cajoles with a smile. "You've been to several of our weddings. Are they not righteously epic?"

"There's no disputing they are, but Katie and I have some important business we need to settle first. If there is one thing I learned from Elyssa's death, you have to put the past away before you can move on to the future."

A pained look crosses Tara's face. "I can't argue with you. Just be careful the past doesn't derail your future."

"Now that we have talked about the great news regarding your trip, why don't you tell us the rest of the story?" Nick says as he studies both of us. "I have a feeling there was much more to your visit than going back to see your brother get married, right?"

I sigh. "It looks like the authorities have identified a potential suspect. However, no one is exactly sure where he's at or what he is capable of doing."

Tasha frowns. "So they know who this guy is? Who is it?"

"He's the brother of the guy I shot and killed during my officer involved shooting." Katie rolls her shoulder.

Jude pipes up, "Not good. It means this is personal, very personal."

"Do you need more manpower?" Aidan asks me.

"Always. You know that. I haven't had a chance to bring anyone else on board yet."

"Why don't you make it your priority? I don't want to leave any members of our team unprotected — especially you Katie."

Katie smiles gratefully at Aidan. "Thank you so much. I wish I was not your burden. It isn't fair if you have to spend more money because I am part of the team."

Tara walks up to Katie and puts her hand on her shoulder as she says, "One thing I have learned about being a crime victim is life is rarely fair — I learned that the hard way. You have to play the hand you're dealt. Fortunately, we have the resources to do this. I don't want you to give it a second thought."

"I can't tell you how much I appreciate that. Hopefully, this nightmare will be over soon and my team members back in Florida will find whoever this is."

Tara shrugs. "That would be the optimal outcome, but don't let your guard down. Unfortunately, I have experience being in your shoes. It's not fun."

"We know. We've been watching our backs pretty closely — but it doesn't seem to be enough."

It's amazing how much paperwork can stack up when you're gone for a few days. I'm trying to shuffle it all when my phone rings.

"Hello? Silent Beats, how can I help you?" I answer without glancing at the phone.

"Logan? This is Tristan. Is Katie around? I can't seem to connect with her cell phone."

"No, I'm sorry. She and Tasha went to go visit some kids at the hospital. It's possible she is in a place with no reception. Is there anything I can do for you?" I ask as my heart rate ratchets up.

"I debated whether I should call you, but I have an odd gut feeling about this," Tristan admits.

"You know I can't keep my people safe unless I know the whole situation," I challenge.

"That's precisely why I erred on the side of caution," Tristan says with a sigh.

"What's the SITREP?" I revert back to my military vernacular.

Tristan hesitates. "I'm not exactly sure I have a situation to report on. This is like catching a spiderweb. I called you because they were pinging Coggin's phone for a while, and then it just dropped off. At this point, no one knows where he is. Apparently, he has stopped using all traceable forms of ID or currency. He's not using any of his known bank accounts or credit cards. It is possible he has gone way underground. Of course, it's also possible he has an awful case of food poisoning and just isn't active right now."

"Tristan, you guys have been in this game for a long time. What does the rest of the team think?" I demand impatiently.

Tristan sighs again. "Well, I'm on the phone with you, aren't I? I can't make an official recommendation because I am a consultant on the task force, but something about this feels off to me. So, I'm giving you a head's up just in case."

"Thank you, I appreciate your candor and professional judgment. I will take the appropriate precautions."

"I hope I'm wrong and it's nothing — but you never know."

"Understood." Emotion colors my voice. "You can never be too careful."

"10-4, if it were Rogue, I would probably react the same way. Stay safe, will you?"

"I'll give it my best shot," I reply.

"Okay, I'll be in touch another time," Tristan says as the phone goes dead.

I sink back into my leather executive chair after I check Jude's phone. I know he still has his cell phone on because he sent me a text message about the number of paparazzi out in front of the hospital. As I confirm the GPS location, everyone on my team is where they are supposed to be. I breathe a sigh of relief but I know it's only temporary. I have to make a few decisions about the composition of the team in order to keep Katie safe.

Aidan pokes his head into my office and sets a pile

of papers on my desk. "These are the authorization for background checks. For some reason, they got put on my desk instead of yours." He turns to leave my office but pauses for a moment before he asks, "Is everything okay?"

I rake my hand through my hair. "No, not really."

At my simple declaration, Aidan comes and sits on my couch. "Lay it on me. I know it's gotta be something big. Your face says it all."

"It seems like the threat against Katie might be getting closer to us. They lost the suspect, and they can't make any guarantees he is not on the West Coast."

"That complicates things," Aidan remarks. "What will you do?"

"I'm pulling her off the front line. She doesn't need to be exposed to the public right now. We have to keep closer tabs on her."

Aidan looks at me with wide-eyed astonishment. "Have you actually met your fiancé?"

His term takes me by surprise — not that Katie and I are engaged, but the formality of it. This is the first time I've ever heard anybody use that term with me; it sounds weird when it's vocalized.

I glance at Aidan blankly. "Of course I know my fiancé."

"Then the shock of the situation must've gone to your head because you are not thinking this through."

"What are you saying?" I try to focus on the conversation while frightening thoughts are racing through my head.

"You and I are in love with strong women who like

to fight their own battles. I can't imagine Katie wants you to shelter her in a cocoon. After all, she is a trained professional."

I get up from my chair and pace in front of my window.

Aidan's words make me stop in my tracks as my stomach takes a dive. "You know, you're right. I didn't even think about that; I was so intent on protecting her. She won't want to be pulled off the front line. She is too much of a warrior. Have you ever seen how competitive we are? She can out shoot me at the range any day of the week."

"That's what I'm saying. I had the same issue when Tara wanted to confront her attacker. I wanted to wrap her up in cotton and stick her in a castle somewhere like some Disney princess, but she wasn't having any of it. In the end, I'm glad she confronted Warren Jones. It made all the difference in the world."

"The circumstances are different though, she confronted Warren Jones in a courtroom. However, this Coggins guy is presumably armed and dangerous. He's got nothing else to lose because he's already been caught by his DNA."

"I agree. You are in an untenable situation. I don't think there is a winning formula. You have to make some tough choices."

"What am I supposed to do?" I ask, feeling helpless. "Any decision I make could be dangerous to someone. I don't want to lose my relationship over this."

"I would highly suggest you talk to Katie before you make any unilateral moves. If you try to move her around like a pawn on a chessboard, she will go ballistic on you."

"You're not wrong." I sigh. "Tristan is waiting for service records on a candidate I interviewed the other day. I like this kid. His name is Blake Adams. I think he would make an excellent addition to our team. His MOS was 31 bravo."

"You'll have to translate that into non-military speak for me," Aidan instructs.

"Oh, sorry. It means he was former military police. From what I've seen, his creds look good. But I'll let Tristan and Isaac do the deep diving into his record to make sure everything is on the up and up. But, man, oh man do I wish this was already done. I could use some help to watch Katie's six."

"I'll call Tristan and see if we can work around the hold-up. I want you to have enough people here to do your job."

"I do too. But I'd rather not put Katie in harm's way."

"With all due respect, you didn't put her in harm's way, she made the choice to be there."

I heave a heavy sigh. "I understand what you mean, but still, I promised her family I would take good care of her. In my mind, that means keeping her out of the line of fire."

"You're preaching to the choir, but I have a feeling Katie won't feel the same. Consider yourself forewarned."

I nod. "Duly noted."

"I'm sure I must've misheard you. You couldn't possibly be asking me to stand down from this case, right?" Katie levels as she scowls at me.

"I hate to do this, but I need to keep you safe," I answer reflexively.

"Well, how about you let me do my job! You know, the one I was trained to do and the one you hired me for?"

"I don't know if that's such a good idea. There is a target on your back. Like literally. This guy is escalating. You can't argue with that."

"Of course I'm not going to argue," Katie says with exasperation. "I have to know where exactly you think I got my credentials? I didn't get them from a Cracker Jack box. I have a degree in criminal justice and graduated at the top of my police academy. For the record, I didn't even let them water down the requirements of the physical tests because I wanted to compete one on one with my classmates. Which means, I actually did graduate at the top of my class."

I clench and unclench my fists in frustration as I say, "Katie, I'm not questioning whether you are qualified to do this; clearly you are. The problem is whether you are the right person to do it given the circumstances. As the team leader, my judgment is you're probably not. I don't want to lose people by making poor decisions."

"Then stop making decisions with your emotions and start thinking like this is a mission. I am fully capable of doing my job. It is not your duty to protect me."

"Still, I would rather not —" I argue.

"Logan, when you hired me, you said the reason you were hiring me was because Silent Beats is short on coverage. To take me out would make the problem worse. So, did you really hire me for my skills or did you hire me because you thought I was cute?"

"I suspect if I tell you the truth, you'll probably hit me over the head with my stapler," I admit.

"Why don't you try me?" she crosses her arms in front of her.

"The honest to God's truth is I hired you because you are a bit of both. I know from shooting against you at the range you are a phenomenal shot and you got a ringing endorsement from most of your former colleagues. However, I can't deny I am attracted to you. I have been since day one."

Katie rolls her eyes. "I appreciate your honesty. Truth be told, I only took this job because you're cute," Katie quips as she sticks her tongue out at me. "So, we have established I am a qualified, popular and decorated officer of the law. Let me do my job and we'll be good," she adds with a stern look.

I stretch a kink out of my neck and sigh heavily. "This goes against my gut instinct, but, you make a compelling case. I won't yank your detail. But if you see or feel something unusual, you need to sound the alarm. Do you understand? I'm not talking like your fiancé now. I'm talking as your superior officer."

Katie straightens up and gives me a salute. "Crystal clear. I am here to protect Aidan and his crew. I'll react like the professional I'm trying to be. No hotdogging or cowboying it for me. If something is off, you'll be the first to know."

"I'm not sure if I'm happy or sad we have an agreement on that. An enormous part of me wishes I could keep you away from all of this."

"I know Logan, I'm afraid too. But this is what I

signed up for. We have a job to do."

I stand up and place my arm around her waist as I escort her to the rehearsal room. "As much as I know you are a consummate professional, I will be so glad when all of this is over, and the bad guys are in jail."

She hugs me as she says, "I know. You haven't stopped watching over me from the moment we met. Most of the time I appreciate it."

CHAPTER TWENTY-THREE

KATIE

"LOGAN! GET IN HERE," I practically shout after I hang up the phone with my former partner.

Logan runs into my little office with his weapon half drawn.

When he sees me calmly sitting at my desk holding the telephone, he yells at me, "Way to take several decades off my life. What the heck is going on? Why did you scream my name? We have intercoms, you know."

"What can I say? I got carried away for a moment."

"So, what is the deal?"

"Cody called. They have Vincent in custody. Oh my Gosh! Did I ever dodge a bullet with him —"

"What do you mean?" Logan demands as he examines me carefully. It's like he can't believe I'm in one piece.

"He was brought in on a vice warrant. It seems he was trolling for underage girls on a chat board trying to find someone who would marry him in the next two days. He tried to kidnap one of them."

"Wow, you're right — that is creepy."

"More than you can possibly imagine. I was almost this guy's wife. That's enough to make me want to puke."

"But you're not. You're going to be my wife and we will have a phenomenal, legendary marriage like your parents. Whenever you think about him, remember you and I met because of him."

My eyes tear up. "You always say the sweetest things."

"Thank you. I try. You are inspiring," Logan smiles. Growing more serious, he asks, "What do they make of Coggins as a suspect now they've caught Hurlington?"

"Cody says he doesn't know what to think. Gareth is making the case we should still follow Coggins, but Cody thinks Coggins was a red herring. According to Cody, Coggins could have been a maintenance worker checking my meter."

"Does he have anything in his background indicating he might have access to your house?"

"His employment record indicates he is a mid-level executive at an alternative energy company. It is possible his company is the one who supplies my natural gas."

Logan rubs the back of his neck as he does when he is trying to puzzle out a problem. "I suppose that could technically be true — it would help explain the leather work gloves that go all the way up the arm — maybe they were industrial."

"All I know is I'm breathing a huge sigh of relief. I worried about Vincent from the time he blew a gasket at our wedding; he looked positively unhinged. This development with him does not surprise me as much as it probably should."

"From everything I've studied about your case, I think you're right. I think something inside his head flipped when he was cornered financially. I still think this is all related to money. I don't think he intentionally meant to target you. I think any woman probably would've done, as long as they agreed to marry him. I suspect he targeted you because you fit the mold of someone he could see as a wife."

A shiver goes up my spine and my voice shakes when I challenge, "I don't know, his motives never made sense. He invested tons of time in making us work, and then suddenly made all these demands on me, I thought maybe that was the way it was supposed to go. Until I met you, I had never been in love with anyone; it's crazy. I thought his behavior was normal."

Logan stands up and crosses the office to give me a hug and whisper in my ear, "I can't tell you how glad I am you are safe. I've worried about you every second of every day since I saw you tossing back the Jack Daniels on your wedding day."

I raise my head and kiss him as I kick my office door shut. "I have to admit, it feels good to take a deep breath for a change and be able to think about moving on with my life. If I don't say it often enough, thank you for rescuing me from myself that night."

Logan winks at me. "All in a day's work."

An alarm goes off on my phone. "Speaking of work, you and I have a security assignment at the Children's Museum to benefit Doernbecker's."

"I'll go get Jude and Tasha from the recording booth. Last I checked, they were working on a new duet together. Do you want to get Mindy?"

"Is she still writing a song with Jerome?" I ask.

"That's where I last saw her when I made rounds,"

Logan confirms.

"I'll get her. Do you want to take the black SUV or the navy one?"

"I prefer the black one. Do you want me to park by the East entrance?"

"Yeah, I will angle my rig toward the North. In case we need to make a quick exit."

Giving him one last quick kiss, I say, "It's a plan, partner."

I unlock the parking garage and grab Mindy's guitar. "Are you ready for this? The ones with kids are always so emotional."

Mindy puts her hand on my shoulder to stop me from leaning into the vehicle. "I know I am the person you are protecting, but please listen to me when I tell you we all need to ride together. The SUV is big enough for us to do that."

I stand up and study the expression on Mindy's face. She is somber and there is a frightened look in her eyes. She has never made a prediction involving me before, but I have heard countless stories about her skills as well as Tara's. Her expression is enough to make me stop and radio Logan.

"Did you lose her already?" he asks in an amused voice.

I hold my radio up to my ear. "No, Mindy's right here. I have a question. Mouse wants to combine rigs — do you have any objection?"

There is a decided pause on the other end of the

radio. "I guess that's all right. It's a pretty small venue. I'll swing around and pick you guys up."

"Works for me," I answer as I pick up Mindy's guitar.

"Thank you for listening to me," Mindy responds in a subdued voice.

"Hey, it's no problem. The SUVs are gas guzzlers anyway. One less vehicle on the road couldn't hurt anything."

As Logan pulls up in front of me, he rolls down the window. "Ladies, your chariot has arrived."

Mindy walks around the vehicle to sit next to Logan. "I hope you don't mind. I get carsick when I ride in the back," she asks looking at me.

"No, I don't mind. I'm short enough I don't need the legroom. Besides, somebody needs to supervise these lovebirds in the back here!" I joke with a wink.

Jude looks up. "I don't think we need a chaperone, we're old enough to do everything you and Logan are doing."

I close my eyes. "Point taken. Carry on. Just don't get arrested for indecent exposure or anything — I don't have bail money."

Tasha yawns. "I think I'll take a nap. Wake me up when we get to Portland."

Jude smirks at me. "See how quickly the romance wears off? My girlfriend would rather take a nap than cuddle with me. It's sad to see the bloom of love drop off so quickly."

Tasha looks at Jude with wide-eyed surprise. "I can't believe you would say that. The reason I'm so tired is because a hot up-and-coming rock star I know kept me awake all night last night."

"Eww!" Mindy makes face and plugging her ears "TMI much?"

Tasha blushes. "Sorry, Mindy. I forget not everyone is in a relationship like mine."

Mindy looks back at Tasha. "That's all right. I fully expect to be alone for my whole life so, I'll have to get used to it one way or another."

Mindy's statement puzzles me. "What makes you so sure you'll be alone? You are still very young. I think it's a little early to determine that."

"I know you haven't been around long, but I am the definition of weird, strange, and oddball."

"I don't think so," I answer as I examine the tall willowy teenager.

She shrugs. "It's true. I've accepted it."

"Well, you never know what will happen," I advise sagely.

Mindy sighs softly. "The problem is I do know. But it's okay, I've had a long time to get used to the fact I'm different."

"Yeah, Mindy I wouldn't worry about it," Tasha responds. "Look what happened with Jude and me — he practically hated my guts when we met, but now he's my biggest supporter. Great things can happen with you too. Wait and see what fate has in store for you."

Mindy shrugs elegantly. "I guess only time will tell." She turns to Jude. "Do you want to work on our song? I brought the iPad."

Jude shrugs. "As long as Tasha is sleeping, I might as well do some songwriting. What are you working on?"

"It's a little hard without my guitar, but I think I can hum it for you."

"Okay, we'll try to work with that. You have pretty good pitch so it shouldn't be too much of a problem."

Logan pulls out into traffic and starts up I-5 toward Portland. I dig the Kindle out of my purse and start to read. Soon I get sleepy too. "Do you mind if I catch a little shuteye?" I ask Logan as my eyes droop.

"Nope, not a problem. I'll let you know when we get to the outskirts of Portland. This drive is pretty boring."

After a while, the car slows to a stop. I open my eyes and glance over Logan's shoulder to see if I can figure out what's going on. He hears me shuffle in the back and explains, "Stupid traffic on '26. I don't know why I'm never prepared for it. I guess I have turned into a small-town guy since working for Aidan. Traffic drives me nuts."

I peer out the window. "Is it always this bad? I thought Florida roads were terrible, but it seems like you all are giving us a run for our money."

"Imagine making this trip on a school bus. It's miserable. I like the museums, but the trip is awful," Mindy says. I watch as she carefully tucks her iPad away in her bag. "Thank goodness we are almost —"

Without warning, something hits the driver side window. "Take cover!" I shout as a guy holds a 9mm aimed straight at Logan's ear.

Instinctively, I dive forward in my seat and shove Logan over to the side as I draw my weapon and fire it. I don't even have time to think through the physics of deflection — or anything else for that matter. I follow through with three more shots to make sure the suspect is down. *Crap! I sure could use Cody to be my backup right now.* The window explodes violently, showering Logan and me with tiny shards of glass. Some of it flies toward my face, making it difficult for me to see if the suspect is down.

"Am I clear?" Logan shouts as he lays on the seat covering Mindy with his body.

My vision finally clears and I try to assess the situation while staying away from the window. To say it is awkward is an understatement. My heart is racing like a tattoo machine.

"Oh my Gosh! How does that happen? Someone shot at us in the middle of the highway!" Tasha exclaims breathlessly.

"Logan, I don't see him. Unless he is a ghost, he is 10-39."

Logan sits up slowly and brushes the glass off himself. "Wow! You not only pushed me out of the way, but you also got the perp."

I laugh shakily. "You still want to plant me on a desk somewhere?"

"Heck no! Obviously, that was the worst idea I ever had. You are welcome to watch my six anytime," Logan says in a voice riddled with emotion.

"I plan on it. That's why I said yes,"

"I hate to break this up, but I called the police in case you all want some assistance figuring out what's going on," Jude announces as he shows me his cell phone.

Logan swallows hard. "Way to keep a level head. I'm not thinking clearly right now. I am still trying to process everything. Katie, you saved my life, without a doubt."

I wipe some sweat off my brow. "Well, there were a

lot of people who helped me get better at this job. One of them was my firearms instructor. I think I'll probably send him a whole box of lottery tickets. After all, I think we probably used up our luck for a while."

"I feel responsible. I was too quick to dismiss the possibility of another suspect after Hurlington was arrested."

"Having been there, done that recently — very recently — you cannot do this to yourself. There is enough blame to go around and all of it goes on the guy laying on the ground."

"I know, but I'm sorry I put you in this position," Logan laments. I notice his hands are shaking as much as mine.

"Logan — *you* didn't put me in this situation. I only got a quick glimpse of him, but my guess is that's Coggins out there and he met the same fate as his brother."

Logan whistles softly through his teeth. "As I said before, your aim is phenomenal."

I grab a bottle of water from the built-in cooler in the SUV and start to gulp it down. "You do realize you won't get to see me for the next few months because I'm about to be completely buried in paperwork."

"I think we probably all are, but that's better than someone being dead." Tasha asserts.

"True enough. Hopefully this time, I have run out of bad guys who are after me. This is getting really, really old."

Epilogue

Logan

"Can you buckle my shoe?" Katie asks as she sinks a little further into the plush bed and growls in frustration. "I don't know why I listened to Stella and Tasha and got a manicure. I am hopeless when I'm all dressed up. I can't even fasten my own shoes."

Leaning over, I hold her slim ankle in my hands and buckle the impossibly thin strap. "I can understand why you are having trouble. It practically takes an engineering degree to fasten these."

"Speaking of engineering degrees, I can't believe your parents are coming to the ceremony. I'm so happy they are coming as a couple."

My parents' joint attendance at the ceremony was one of the few happy surprises we've had recently. It has been a rough few months. It seemed like the investigation into the shooting kept spawning new investigations. It almost seemed like it would never end.

"I know. I am grateful to see them together. It always made me profoundly sad to think of them apart," I comment. "I hope you know how proud my parents are of your takedown. You can't even imagine how much my mother brags on you to all her friends. My dad is not far behind."

Katie shoots me an amused smirk. "Has your dad stopped telling people you'd be dead without me in your life? That's how he introduced me when we went to the store to get a newspaper the other day. It was like you had no military or security experience at all. I tried to remind him of all the things you've done in your life, too, but he wouldn't be dissuaded. He kept introducing me to every customer in the little market."

"I don't blame him. I would be dead if you hadn't been there. Kristoph Coggins had me in his sites, there is no escaping it. If you hadn't reacted so quickly, we would be having an entirely different interaction."

She shrugs. "I wish I could take credit for all of it, but instincts kicked in. I did what I had to do to save everyone's lives. When I was in the Academy, I used to do all sorts of extra training modules no one ever thought I'd need. I did it to sharpen my skills and to make sure I could have clean shots and not take out any innocent victims along the way. I got good at running the scenarios and sorting the bad guys from the innocent bystanders. I never figured I would have to do it in real life. I'm so lucky my shots were not deflected by the window."

"I, for one, am glad you ran all those drills." I caress her ankle.

"All my practice paid off for sure. Not only did the PPD decide it was a clean shot, they thought it was enough for you to get a letter of commendation."

"I know. I was really nervous about facing this whole scenario with the Portland Police Department, but it turned out to be easier than I expected. Maybe because

I'm a civilian now — but either way, it was a lot less trouble than the last one I faced."

"Well, I think it helped your cause a lot that there were other witnesses and your supervisor was right on scene."

"I'm sure it helped. I think what cinched it was the manifesto against me that they found in Coggins' car. I'm not even thirty years old yet, and this guy had one hundred and forty-seven pages worth of garbage to say about me. It was mind-boggling."

"There is that. He was free to make all sorts of accusations against you, but the bottom line is you killed his brother because his brother shot at you after abusing his wife and child. Who knows what pain-and-suffering you saved those two? If Coggins decided to commit suicide-by-cop to send a message about how innocent his brother was, he chose the wrong way to go about it. It is impossible to fix that kind of stupid. You had no choice but to do what you did. Because you did, you saved my life. I don't feel bad at all. In my book, you are as heroic as they come. Period. Full stop."

I pull her up against me and embrace her. I don't think I'll ever take the ability to hold her in my arms for granted. That call was too close. Coggins could have aimed the gun at her just as easily. I came within seconds of losing another person I love. It's a sobering, terrifying thought. I know she would make the same decision to put herself in harm's way to protect me every day of the week. It's who she is and I love her for it — even if it does give me nightmares.

Gently kissing her, I pull her hair out of her eyes and say, "I am so proud of you. You are one of the best body men I've ever seen."

"I'm pretty sure there was a compliment buried in there somewhere," Katie replies with a smile.

"Oh, there was, believe me." I pull away and grab her purse. "What are you going to tell Tyler? I understand he made you a job offer at the Sheriff's Office."

"He did. I don't know what to do about it. For the longest time, all I wanted to be was a police officer working with the public. Working with the Sheriff's Office would allow me to do that. But, you showed me a whole another dream. I like traveling with Aidan and the band. Mindy is one of my favorite people ever. She makes the job fun. When I think about it, it's not just her — it's everyone at Silent Beats. You all feel like my family now. I don't know if I could leave and go work somewhere else."

"So, none of the decision-making process has anything to do with working for me?" I tease.

"Didn't we just have this conversation when you incorrectly assumed I wouldn't be able to protect myself under pressure?"

I look up at the sky and whistle. "Do I have to admit that? I'd like to pretend that conversation never took place."

"Which part of it? The part where you threatened to fire me because I was a victim, or the part where I told you I went to work for you because I thought you were hot?"

"To revisit something else I said that day, 'It's a bit of both'. I'm sorry I doubted your skills. I rather like being your hot boss."

"Touring with Aidan and the rest of the gang is a lifestyle I never thought I would like, but I love it. I love you — which makes this decision excruciatingly hard. I might like working for the Sheriff's office just as much, but I don't know. I could hate it. It could be as stifling and chauvinistic as the place I left before."

I place my arm around her waist, as we walk out to my car in thoughtful silence. Before we get in, I press her up against the side of the car and kiss her again. "I can't decide for you. I would recommend talking to some of Tyler's coworkers and seeing what the political environment of the offices is."

"I've got a few calls in," she admits.

"Good. I need you to know, regardless of what you decide, I support your decision. Do what's right for you."

"For a long time in my career, I wondered if I could get any job and now I have two great jobs offers. I'm not even sure what to think." She lays her chin on my chest and grabs my waist and pulls me closer. "What if I make the wrong choice?" she whispers hoarsely.

"Honestly, Katie you got two excellent choices. I don't think you could go wrong with either one of them. You have to follow your heart."

"What if my heart is in several pieces and I don't know how to make it all makes sense?"

"I'm not a big believer in the world making sense. Sometimes it's chaotic, angry and exciting. You just have to roll with the punches," I declare philosophically.

"— sometimes, rolling with the punches means I'm the happiest I've ever been," Katie finishes my sentence with a tearful smile. It's funny how she took the words right of my mouth.

EPILOGUE

KATIE

THE MINUTE WE PULL up to the bar, my eyes light up. "Revisiting the scene of the crime, are we?" I quip. "You'll excuse me if I don't order any Jack Daniels; I've sworn it off for life."

"Having been there to pick up the pieces after the last time, I fully understand your choice. However, I think you'll find this bar is a cut above the last one you visited. Aidan comes here so often to celebrate; the owners give him an exclusive deal to rent the whole place out. It is so hard for him and Tara to have a regular social life since he hit the top of the charts, they have to be really careful where they go." Logan explains as he helps me with the door.

When we walk in the door, it's reminiscent of the nineteen eighties sitcom where everyone knew your name. Everybody in the place starts to clap.

I look at Logan in surprise. "I thought you said we were coming here for the killer potato skins and football? Why is everybody here?"

Aidan and Tara walk up to us dressed in matching flannel and blue jeans as Tara replies, "Did you forget we promised you a party a few months ago?"

"Honestly, yes I forgot. So much has happened since Logan and I first came to Oregon, time has flown by."

"I heard the judge dismissed the family's case against you for wrongful death."

I move closer to Logan and he sticks his arm around me before I say, "Yes, thank goodness. I think, finally — this time for sure — this whole tragedy is behind me. People think I get some sort of charge by killing people. I really don't. I would much rather have taken another path. But those guys didn't give me a chance. If I see a weapon, I have to shoot."

"Are you under the impression we think you were in the wrong?" Aidan asks. "Because if you are, don't bother. Logan has been one of my best friends in this industry — he's stuck with me for several years now. The fact you saved his life means the world to me."

"I'm sorry, I guess I'm sensitive. I don't know what people think of us law enforcement types anymore. It doesn't seem to matter that I'm providing private security for Silent Beats now. Everybody connects me to the two shootings. It's not something I can escape."

"But you understand it was necessary, right?" Tara asks softly. "I have been the victim of crime before. The people you were dealing with, whether it be the Coggins brothers or Vincent Hurlington, didn't respect who you were as a person, and they violated you too."

"I guess it's hard to refer to myself as a victim, but those two deaths lay on my conscience, so I guess in a way, I really am. Whether I'm a victim of them or a victim of my circumstances, I'm not sure. It sure would be nice to be able to pretend all of this never happened," I explain.

Logan raises an eyebrow. "Nothing? I don't know. I think something spectacular happened the day you were supposed to get married and didn't."

I turn in Logan's arms and slide my hands up his biceps. "Something big did happen to me that day. I found the man who made all the pieces of my life make sense."

Logan takes my hand and drags me up toward the karaoke stage. I try to halt his progress. "Oh, no you don't. I'm not doing karaoke with a room full of professional singers. My self-esteem wouldn't be able to handle it. Besides, John will tell you I am a terrible singer. I have been since the moment I learned what singing was. It's not like I didn't try, but the talent just isn't there," I babble as my heart races and I break out in a cold sweat.

Logan hugs me to him. "Relax. If we want someone to sing, there are plenty of professional singers here to cover the gig. I am not making you do anything you don't want to do. I promise."

From the vantage of the stage, I look out at the dance floor. I smile up at Logan and say, "I might not be able to sing, but I like to line dance."

A familiar smile attracts my notice. "Oh my gosh! What are my parents doing here in Oregon?"

Aidan walks up on stage and hands me a beer. "I thought I told you this is a party. We do parties big here. I don't know if you can see in this lighting, but your brother and sister-in-law are here too."

"I don't understand," I stammer. "Thank you for bringing my family members here. But, don't you think it's a bit of overkill for an after-work party?"

Tristan walks up behind me. "Lucky for you, Aidan has developed an affinity for private planes too. So, when he wants to spoil people, he can. Consider yourself spoiled," he declares with a chuckle.

I look over at my family. "Did you guys really fly on a private plane? Oh my gosh, I'm so happy you're here. I have no idea why you're here, but still —"

Rogue rolls her eyes at her husband, Tristan. "Always bragging about your private plane … you know, if you weren't such a nice guy, people would get offended."

"What's offensive? I run an odd transportation service that helps people who haven't seen their family in a while," Tristan protests, his hands wide as he pleads innocent.

Rogue looks up at him incredulously. "A transportation service? You own a private plane and you're getting ready to buy a second one. That's more than running your family member to the library on Saturday morning to do homework."

"You know me, I like random acts of kindness."

I smile at Logan. "I like random acts of kindness too — especially when they are performed by big, handsome strangers who pick up poor unsuspecting women in stained wedding dresses and make their lives perfect."

Logan takes a deep breath and sticks his hand in the breast pocket of his jacket. "I'm so glad you said that. Because I would like to make it official. As a result of the drama in our lives recently, we haven't gotten around to do this on the record. So, I worked with Tristan and Aidan to get all the important people in your life together for this."

I want to stamp my feet impatiently. "What is this?"

But, instead I stare at him and concentrate on how relaxing and handsome he is.

Suddenly, Logan drops to one knee. "Katelyn Ann Ashford, everything about our relationship has gone against conventional wisdom and logic. But, so be it. We have always done things together since we met. Even asking each other to marry the other in the same conversation. Sadly, your friends and family and my friends and family could not be there. So will you marry me and pledge your love to me in front of all these people?"

My hand is shaking so hard Logan is having a hard time putting the ring on my finger after I hold out my hand. "I said yes months ago and I still mean it today. I love you so much."

Logan stands and says, "I love you too. Finally, all the pieces in my life fit together and make me whole."

Aidan comes up and claps Logan on the back and shakes my hand as he says, "I'm so glad the two of you found each other. For many years, I watched Logan struggle with his past. It is nice to see the two of you looking forward to the future." He looks over at Tara and then back at us as he says, "Okay, I've made my little speech, let's have some fun."

"It sounds like a plan to me," I smile. "I am ready to put my past behind me."

When Aidan looks over in the corner, I realize there is a DJ sitting at a small station. Aidan instructs, "Let the party begin in honor of love and togetherness."

As a country song plays, everyone goes into the middle of the dance floor. When I say everyone, I mean everyone. Logan's parents are here, and so are his sisters.

My parents are here along with my brother. Almost every employee of Silent Beats is here too. This is the most amazing thing I've ever seen in my life. Suddenly, I get emotional. Without even thinking, I say, "I wish Florida was not so far away from Oregon. I like having everyone together."

Tristan grins. "That's what planes, trains and automobiles are for. Fortunately for me, I have a rather large obsession with them. I got any means of transportation you'd like. If you want to visit with your family, all you have to do is drop me an email and I'll make it happen."

Teary-eyed I look up at Logan. "How did we get such spectacular friends and family members? Most people aren't this lucky."

"I believe that sums up our relationship quite perfectly."

THE END

The Hidden Hearts Series continues with Darya and Stuart's story in Hearts Set Free.

Note from the Author

Dear Reader,

Thank you so much for reading *Pieces*. I hope you enjoyed reading my unique romance with a bit of mystery thrown in.

The adventures continue in *Hearts Set Free*.

Nobody said police work was easy.

Darya Vick knows this better than most. Her husband was killed by a car bomb. It didn't matter that he was the team leader of his bomb disposal unit. Her daughter never had a chance to know her dad.

Now Darya faces a whole new round of threats.

Can her friend, local veterinarian, Dr. Stuart Eastwood, help her solve a series of baffling cases and keep her daughter safe?

You'll love this romantic story of new beginnings and starting over.

Get *Hearts Set Free* in paperback, e-book edition or read through Kindle Unlimited for free now

Thank you,

~Mary

Because love matters, differences don't.

ACKNOWLEDGEMENTS

When I was a freshman in college, the police academy was located on my college campus. Historically, the students on campus didn't interact much with the people going through police academy training. However, I didn't know about this tradition — so, I invited them to eat lunch with me. I did not know what doors I opened that day with my simple request. I made friendships that day and over the next several weeks that impacted my life for decades. This book is dedicated to those friends and every other police officer who does their job with loyalty and integrity.

It takes a special breed of person to be able to have the perspective to be a good law enforcement officer. You have my gratitude and respect. I realize that in today's political environment, it might be hard for people to say how much they appreciate your dedication. For the people who treat you poorly just for doing your job, I apologize. For those who celebrate the triumph of good over evil, I celebrate with them. Thank you for your service.

It also takes a special kind of courage to live with a disabling condition no one else can see. So, in this book, I acknowledge the struggles of individuals with disabilities which you cannot see. Thank you for being tough and tenacious and fighters when no one can see your battle.

By the time this book is published, my oldest son will be Dr. Crawford. I cannot tell you how proud I am of your accomplishments. Brandon, you have become an honorable, compassionate man. I am proud of the way you take care of your wife and son. You are the kind of person I always dreamed of having as a child. Good luck in your residency.

To my other son, Justin — thank you for your humor and help every day. You make life fun and interesting in ways I never expected. I am proud of you too.

To my husband Leonard – I know that being the spouse of an author is a very large challenge. My mind is often in a whole different world having made up conversations with people you cannot see. Yet, you support me every step of the way. I can't ask for anything more.

One last thank you to the incredible supportive author community. I wish to thank all of you who have taken the time to offer me assistance, guidance and encouragement when all things seemed lost. I love the fact that many authors feel the same way I do — bettering the craft and the people who practice it are important. To foster this belief, you have to put competition on the back burner and cooperation on the front. I want to thank all my friends who have done that with me. May we all sell more books.

~Mary

About the Author

I have been lucky enough to live my own version of a romance novel. I married the guy who kissed me at summer camp. He told me on the night we met that he was going to marry me and be the father of my children.

Eventually, I stopped giggling when he said it, and we've been married for more than thirty years. We have two children. The oldest is a Doctor of Osteopathy. He is across the United States completing his residency, but when he's done, he is going to come back to Oregon and practice Family Medicine. Our youngest son is now tackling high school and where he is an honor student. He is interested in becoming an EMT.

I write full time now. I have published more than thirty books and have several more underway. I volunteer my time to a variety of causes. I have worked as a Civil Rights Attorney and diversity advocate. I spent several years working for various social service agencies before becoming an attorney.

In my spare time, I love to cook, decorate cakes and of course, I obsessively, compulsively read.

I would be honored if you would take a few moments out of your busy day to check out my website,

MaryCrawfordAuthor.com. While you're there, you can sign up for my newsletter and get a free book. I will be announcing my upcoming books and giving sneak peeks as well as sponsoring giveaways and giving you information about other interesting events.

If you have questions or comments, please E-mail me at Mary@MaryCrawfordAuthor.com or find me on the following social networks:

Facebook: www.facebook.com/authormarycrawford

Website: MaryCrawfordAuthor.com

Twitter: www.twitter.com/MaryCrawfordAut